Is It That Obvious??

Chapter 1: Alayah

"Luca? Luca, open the door," I said, knocking on my best friend's door down the hall. I sighed, pulled out my phone, and texted him, "Knock, knock." He didn't answer, but shortly after, the door swung open.

"Sorry," he said to me, "I couldn't hear you." I followed him into his apartment in my socks, a red plaid throw blanket around my shoulders. When he faced me again, I signed in ASL.

"Why don't you have your aid in?" I signed and spoke at the same time.

"You know I hate this thing," he signed back, then picked up his hearing aid from the kitchen counter and placed it in his ear.

Even though we were only in our mid-twenties, Luca had lost most of his hearing already due to a genetic disorder that ran in his family. He wasn't completely deaf, though, at least not yet. It happened gradually. He could still hear a little bit, but that's what the hearing aids were for. Although, he only wore one most of the time, in his left ear. He refused to wear both at the same time, ever since this mean kid in middle school called him an "old man." It was something he was still insecure about.

"Well, you need it. So wear it," I said out loud while still signing, then I laughed a little, "How are you gonna tell me to come over and then not hear me knock?"

"Sorry, Lay! Geez," he laughed, too, "I forgot." He plopped down on the futon couch and resumed his video game on the tv. I sat next to him and took out my phone for some mindless scrolling.

Luca and I had always been close friends since we were kids, our families were close. But, he and I didn't become *best* friends until early high school. I was the only one that knew ASL, so his parents requested that we'd be put in all the same classes. We spent a lot of time together because of it, goofing around and sneaking snacks in class, riding the bus home and doing our homework at each other's houses. We went to prom together junior and senior year, and had been close ever since.

Now granted, I was not perfect at signing at the time at all. I only knew the basics beforehand. But, his mother also had the same disorder, so I learned a lot from them both over time. I was fluent now. Sometimes Luca and I spoke in ASL just for fun whether he had his aids in or not, especially when we were around other people.

We talked about anything, told each other everything. He was quite literally my best friend. And now

7

—conveniently—we lived in the same apartment complex, just a few doors apart on the same floor. I was 303 and he was 307. And we were always back and forth, bothering each other and getting on each other's nerves. More times than not, people always thought that we were a couple because we were so close, but Luca and I had never thought of each other that way.

"How's Liz?" I asked him, reaching over to the tin of Pringles sitting on the small coffee table.

"I haven't seen her in a few days, but she's good. Wracking her brain with nursing school," he told me, shooting zombies on the tv screen. Elizabeth was his fiancée. They had been together for three years total and engaged for three months.

"Oh, that's right. I remember her saying that when we all went bowling a few weeks ago," I said back, wrapping myself back up in my throw blanket as I crunched on a few chips.

"Yeah, the same day Cameron decided to show up late and we had to pay for extra time to keep our lane," Luca said back, glancing at me with slight agitation.

"Okay, that wasn't his fault. He got off work late," I said back, rolling my eyes.

"Alayah, he's terrible," Luca chuckled, turning his attention back to the tv, "He does that to you all the time."

"I think you just don't like him," I mumbled. He shook his head, but didn't say anything else.

Cameron was my boyfriend. We had been on and off for five years. He could be very sweet when he wanted to, but other times he was more nonchalant and distant than I would've liked. When we were 'on', things would be okay. When we were 'off', we dated other people just to end up back together anyway. It was complicated, honestly.

But over the years, I had grown to love him and it was hard to stay mad at him.

Luca didn't like him very much. He never had, even from the beginning. But, sometimes the four of us would go on double dates or just hang out all together, and I always had to remind Luca to be nice. Not that he would ever say anything, but he was not very good at hiding his disdain for Cameron with the expressions on his face. I wasn't sure if Cameron knew Luca wasn't fond of him or not. I think he knew. We only went on those double dates occasionally because it was Liz's idea, way for all of us to hang out together. But other than those times, Luca and Cameron didn't talk much.

The fighting and graphics on Luca's game got louder and more intense. He sat up and locked in his focus. I scrolled more on my phone, occasionally popping up to show him memes and videos.

"How did work go? Is your computer alright now?" He asked me after a while.

"Yeah, I didn't have any problems today," I replied, "Just annoying people per usual. Love getting yelled at over the phone." Luca laughed a little, eyes still on the tv.

I worked from the comfort of my apartment with a remote job from an insurance company, and Luca was my personal IT guy when I had issues. He was actually an IT person at his own job, so that just made it even better for me because I was *not* tech savvy whatsoever. Not when it came to computers. He also had the lovely opportunity to work from home.

Most people nowadays did, ever since a wild unknown virus came and swept through in March. It was April now, and things were chaotic outside, so a lot of people—Luca and I included—barely went anywhere or hung out with anyone else besides each other and our significant others. A lot of places and businesses were closed down anyway, so there wasn't much to do even if we could.

"You need a new job," he said to me. I thought for a second.

"No, cause I love staying at home too much. And I come annoy you when I need a change of scenery," I said.

"Jokes on you, because you don't annoy me," he joked back, looking at me again. He paused the game and shoved a couple Pringles in his mouth, then got up and walked the few steps it took to get over to the kitchen area.

His black framed glasses slipped off his nose a little as he looked down to grab a can of soda from the refrigerator. He tossed me one and I caught it with both hands.

"Now I can't open that right away or it'll explode. Why would you throw it?" I asked and he laughed.

"Oh, my gosh. Shut up. Be happy I thought to grab you one at all," he said, walking back over to the futon.

"First you ignore me knocking on the door, now you're throwing cans at me and being mean," I joked, shaking my head, "Just rude. *You* asked *me* to come over."

"Actually, I said '*are* you coming over?' And you said yes and I said okay," he laughed, "So, technically."

"I don't deserve this," I mumbled, still playing around, and he laughed at me again.

I slouched down in my seat and turned my attention back to my phone. Occasionally I looked up when the video game got interesting as we talked, even though I had seen him play this game a thousand times before. One of his favorite ones.

Most of the time, our days consisted of just this. Even long before the pandemic and working from home, hanging out a lot was always a thing for us. From childhood to high school to college to now, that was just the type of friendship we had.

Chapter 2: Luca

    I hadn't seen my fiancée, Liz, in a few days. I only really saw her a day or two out of the week nowadays anyway. She'd be studying and taking classes online during the day while I was working, and by the time I got off, she would already be gone to her part time job at a Target down the road. And she wasn't too fond of leaving her place if she didn't have to, even if it was coming over to me. So, I usually went over to her, which wasn't a problem. But, she still lived with her parents and her younger sister, so we didn't get much (real) alone time.

    I sat with her in her room, watching some movie she picked from Netflix. She wasn't much of a talker, and neither was I. In that way, we understood each other, being comfortable in silence counted as spending time with each other just as much as doing anything else would.

We actually met at her job a few years back, after she bumped into me while stocking shelves. I immediately thought she was gorgeous, with her long, jet back, hair and pale blue eyes. But I was too shy to say anything at first. I went to Target six more times that week, almost going broke buying stuff I didn't need just to see if she'd be there.

I remember sitting out in the parking lot of the store, mentally preparing myself to go in, practicing what I would say if I saw her. And Alayah was in the passenger seat every one of those days, giving me a pep talk so that I'd feel more confident going for it. But when my shyness stifled me still, Alayah marched over to Liz and told her I was interested in her, right in the electronics section of the store. I thought Liz would've thought I was lame, but I saw her smile, and she gave her number to Alayah to give to me. We had been together ever since.

But lately, things had been a little different. I was sure that it was just the isolation that was making everything weird, and I was hopeful that when all this passed, we would be good again.

She was quiet as she cuddled up to me, head on my chest and her legs intertwined with mine. The glow of the tv on top of her dresser lit up most of the room, other than a small lamp to the right of her. I sunk down a little lower in the bed and pulled her closer to me. She looked up at me with an eyebrow raised.

"My parents are downstairs," she reminded me.

"I know that," I laughed a little, "I wasn't insinuating anything." She looked at me like she didn't believe me.

"Are you sure? Because…you're telling on yourself," she said, lightly tapping her hand below my belt. I laughed again.

"I know your parents are downstairs, Lizzie. I promise that's not what I was doing," I said back to her, "but it would be a lot easier if we just went back to my apartment."

"I already told you I'm not going over there right now," she said, dropping her head back to my chest, "You live around too many people."

"What is the difference?" I asked, somewhat amused by her logic.

"If I go over there, then I'm breathing in everyone's air that passed through the lobby. You coming over here is different," she explained. I still didn't understand, but I let her have it.

I had tried to convince her way too many times already that she should not only come over, but just move in with me. But she insisted she didn't want to do that until we could save up for a bigger place. I guess I understood that, but it would've been nice to be close to her all the time and not just 1.5 days out of the week.

I stayed with her until almost midnight before I left to go home. Even though I worked from home, I still had to get up pretty early and the drive back was a good ten to fifteen minutes. Liz walked with me outside to my car, and lingered a little before saying goodnight.

"Hey, I don't want you to think I don't want to," she said to me, running her fingers through my hair, "It's just my parents are always home and I'm not comfortable going to—"

"Lizzie, you don't have to explain yourself to me. I get it," I told her, admiring the way her olive-toned skin glowed from the streetlights.

"I love you," she said, her voice rising with a bit of cheerfulness to make me feel better, I guess.

"I love you, too," I said back. I grabbed her hands and pulled her close to me, and I kissed her lips. She smiled and scrunched her nose, something she always did after a kiss and I thought it was adorable.

"Be safe," she said, as I hopped in the driver's seat of my car. I assured her I would, and then I drove off.

*****

The next day after work, I walked down the hall to Alayah's and knocked on her door. Bass from whatever music she was playing was making the doorknob vibrate. I knocked again a little louder in case she couldn't hear me the first time, and texted her, "knock, knock." The music got quiet.

"Sorry, I was dancing," she said when she finally opened the door.

"Aren't you always?" I teased her, and she made a face at me.

"Ha, ha. You're not funny," she said back, letting me in.

Alayah had always been a musical person. She was a regular in all the school plays when we were kids and in high school, and she took all types of dance classes on the weekends, even in college. She had a beautiful singing voice, too, but she rarely ever sang in front of me unless she wasn't being serious. She always said it was somehow easier to sing on a stage where she couldn't see anyone's particular face, rather than singing directly for someone. I didn't see the difference, especially because every show she was in, I was front row watching her anyway.

Nowadays, she still randomly bursted into spontaneous performances like it was second nature to her. And there were countless times when she would grab me and insist I dance with her, but I was the complete opposite of her in that aspect. I was a horrible dancer, born without any kind of rhythm whatsoever, but she never cared.

"I thought we were playing *Jenga* today," I said to her, holding up the board game in my hand as I walked in.

"Oh, we are," she said competitively, "I didn't know what time you were coming over. I was wasting time."

We settled in the middle of the floor in the living room and she took the game box from me, dumping everything out. We stacked the wooden blocks up, immediately getting into the game. She rolled up the sleeves of her crewneck sweatshirt and sat crisscrossed, locking in her focus as she silently decided which block to pull first. I laughed at her.

"You lost last time," I reminded her, trying to distract her, "You're gonna lose again."

"Luca, I don't have time for your terrible trash talking right now," she said unfazed, not even looking up at me. I laughed again. Her first pull was steady, and so was mine. We went back and forth, the tower getting more shaky as the minutes went by. Alayah took another piece out and her eyes widened as the blocks tipped just a little, but didn't fall down. She let out a triumphant, "Ha!" I shook my head, taking my turn again next.

"You better watch it, Lay," I teased her, carefully sliding another block out successfully. She laughed and repositioned herself so that she was laying on her stomach, eye level to the floor to deepen her focus. She bit her lip in concentration, her hands steady as she picked her next piece. The tower swayed precariously, and then it finally toppled over, all the blocks crashing to the floor.

"No!" Alayah shouted dramatically, collapsing her head in defeat.

"Face it, Alayah," I told her, laughing, "You can't beat me."

"I want a rematch!" She demanded, her fluffy, curly hair flowing as she popped up.

"Alright," I said, already starting to stack the pieces again, "But if you lose this time, you owe me a ten dollar bill."

"The best I can do is quarters for the washer and dryer," she said back with a shrug, and it made me laugh again.

"It's a bet," I told her. She laughed menacingly, as if she would win this time with money involved. Then, we started the game over.

Chapter 3: Alayah

I went over to my boyfriend, Cameron's apartment a few blocks down after work a couple days later. He worked late the past couple days so I hadn't seen him, but when I got there, it still seemed like I wasn't seeing him. He was on his phone the entire time we were supposed to be watching a movie. Every time I spoke, I had to repeat myself because he wasn't listening the first time.

I think he had become too comfortable, honestly. We had been together (on and off) for so long that he was just... I don't know. But, he wasn't always so careless. Actually when I first met him, he was the most romantic person. Literally worshiped the ground I walked on seemed like. Now? That "honeymoon" phase was over, I guess.

"It's end credits already?" Cameron asked as the movie ended. I just looked at him, annoyed.

"Yeah, and you didn't watch a single part of it," I said back, crossing my arms.

"Aw, baby, I'm sorry," he said, leaning over to kiss me. I rolled my eyes.

"Yeah, yeah, yeah," I said sarcastically. He continued to kiss me until we gradually leaned back on his bed. He hovered over me, forehead to forehead, trying to get something started, but I really wasn't feeling it.

"Can I make it up to you?" He smirked, his deep voice dropping even lower. I looked up at him, and wrapped my arms around his neck. For some stupid reason, I couldn't pass him up.

"I guess," I said back, pulling him a little closer to me. He leaned down and kissed my lips again, then my neck.

"Hold on tight," he smirked, putting my hands on top of his shoulder-length dread locs. I giggled as he slid down under the blanket.

As inattentive as he was lately, he was still great in bed, which was probably part of the reason I always took him back after a breakup. I hadn't quite found anyone else who did things like he did. But this time, it was rather quick and unsatisfying.

After whatever that first round was, I tried to get a second one going—I was far from done—but he shrugged me off.

"I'm tired now," he said, "I haven't seen you in a while. I put my all into that one."

"Seriously?" I said, annoyed again. If that was his "all", then I was very concerned. He nodded and drank from a water bottle from the nightstand.

"I gotchu in like an hour," he promised, picking up his phone again.

20

"I don't want in an hour. I want it now," I said back, crawling on his lap. I rubbed his chest a little and kissed him. He laughed, then grabbed me by my waist to slide me back off of him.

"You gotta relax," he said, focused on replying to a text message. Okay. Now I was irritated. I got up, threw my sweatshirt back on and went to the bathroom. I peed and washed my hands, then wet my hair a little to try and tame my curls back down from all the...activity. By the time I came back out to the bedroom, he was asleep. That fast.

"You gotta be kidding," I gritted through my teeth. I picked up the rest of my clothes and put them on. I thought about waking him up, but I didn't have the energy. I grabbed my phone and my bookbag-style purse, and left out to drive back home.

"Knock, knock," I texted Luca from outside his door. He opened it and let me in right away.

"Can I ask you something?" I asked immediately as I walked in. Luca laughed at me.

"Hi, how are you? I'm good, thanks for asking," he said jokingly.

"Luca, I'm serious," I said after an exasperated sigh. He chuckled again and leaned over the kitchen counter.

"What's wrong?" He asked.

"Am I an idiot or something? Do I have 'doormat' on my forehead? I'm not understanding," I started, pacing around the room, "He's so annoying, I could spit. And like, I guess nothing bad really happened, but like, he barely talked to me the whole time I was over there. I haven't seen him in days and he surely didn't text or call me consistently over those days either, and that's the greeting I get? A half watched movie and quick sex? Am I missing something!?"

21

"At least you're getting sex," he said back, "Liz won't do anything with her parents in the house and they never leave."

"Yeah, that's rough," I said, thinking about the dilemma, "Why don't you drive down the street and do it in the car or something?"

"Cause she refuses to do that, too," Luca replied.

"Yikes. Miss Girl has to lighten up a little," I said to him, and he chuckled a little. "Well, you know what you gotta do," I continued, but he looked at me confused. I gestured a suggestive up-and-down motion with my hand, and Luca just shook his head at me. I laughed out loud hysterically.

"Lay, I think you need to go sit outside. The lockdown is melting your brain," he said to me.

"Okay, but seriously! How long is she gonna make you wait? All the hotels around here are closed, too. She's just gonna have to apologize to her parents later," I said, "You gotta do what you gotta do." Luca just shrugged and changed the subject.

"As for Cameron," he said after a second, "I think he's trash and that you could find literally anyone that's better for you than whatever he's doing."

"You're just saying that because you don't like him," I said back, but he gave me a condescending glance.

"Alayah, do *you* even like him at this point?" He laughed a little, "All you ever do is talk about how he doesn't treat you the same. Why are you still with him?"

"You want me to break up with him?" I asked. He stood up straight and drummed his hands on the surface of the counter.

"No," he said, but I could tell that's not what he really wanted to say, "But I do think you deserve better." A part of me wanted to agree with him, but there was still something deep down that still had a soft spot for Cameron. Like I said, he wasn't always so negligent, but I knew he would come back around. Especially whenever this virus blew over, I was confident our relationship would be okay.

Even though Luca hated my boyfriend, I was still appreciative that he let me rant and vent to him about everything. But we always talked to each other about everything, that was nothing new. There were times throughout the years where we would just sit and talk for hours, judgement free. Luca knew things about me that I didn't even tell my girl friends, and I'd like to think that there were certain things only I knew about him, too. It was nice that I could count on him. I always could.

Chapter 4: Luca

    Liz called me a week later to tell me that she was sick and had to quarantine for fourteen days before I could come back over. Apparently, her younger sister started showing symptoms first and now they all had it. So, that was a turn of events. She still texted me here and there, and I called her at night. I attempted to FaceTime her throughout the day but she always declined those calls, saying she didn't want me to see her looking so "rough".

    "Lizzie, I don't care about all that. I wanna see your face," I told her one day as she held the camera told her ceiling.

    "No, Luke," she said back. She and my parents were the only ones who called me that. "I look like I'm dying."

"Okay, well, in sickness and in health and til death do us part, right?" I joked, and I thought she was going to laugh, but she didn't. We had only been engaged for three months so far, but usually she seemed happy talking about it. Apparently she was too sick for a laugh, though, so I moved on.

"Do you need anything? I can have something delivered over to you," I told her. She coughed violently for a second.

"No, I'm fine. It's okay, don't worry yourself about it" her voice said, camera still pointed upwards.

"Well, I'm gonna worry about you, Lizzie. I want you to get better so I can see you," I told her. Again, she didn't say anything back for a moment.

"I'll call you back later, okay?" She said.

"Sure. I love you," I sighed.

"Love you, too," she replied, then she hung up.

I stood up from my bed and walked out to the kitchen. I wished this lockdown wasn't so…restrictive. Ever since all this started, it was putting a damper on our relationship. It was like her whole attitude shifted, but I could understand. The uncertainty of all the current events and rising numbers of casualties from this virus could make anybody a little off. I was just holding out for when it was all over and I could get back to her.

I opened the cabinets, then the fridge, then the freezer, then the cabinets again. I didn't feel like making anything. I pulled out my phone and texted Alayah.

"Are you busy?" I asked her. She responded almost immediately, probably already scrolling on her phone.

"Nope," she replied.

"Want pizza?" I messaged back.

"Do I want pizza? What kind of question is that. Of course I do. Let's go half," she replied, and I laughed a little to myself. Pizza was her favorite.

"Usual?" I asked.

"Duh! Hopping in the shower first. Be right over," she sent back.

I should've known the number to the pizza place down the street by heart by now, the way Alayah and I constantly ordered food from there. But, I searched it on google and called, getting our usual: large stuffed crust, half pepperoni, half sausage with bread sticks and marinara. They probably knew our names by now.

Alayah came over just as the no-contact delivery of it was done, and carried it in when I opened the door. She sat the big, square box on the kitchen counter with a grin, small water drops falling from the ends of her curls from her shower.

"How much was it? I'll send you half," she said, but I shook my head.

"Don't worry about it," I told her, "but next time it's on you."

"Fine with me!" She said, and flipped the box open. She grabbed a piece from the pepperoni side, but took the pepperoni off because she liked to "save it for later" and continued to eat the slice itself. I pulled a piece from the sausage side and took a bite.

"Liz feeling better?" She asked me after a while.

"I talked to her earlier, she still sounded pretty rough," I told her.

"Gross. I hope she gets over it fast," she said, picking up her pepperoni pieces finally.

"Yeah, I hope so, too, so she can stop being weird," I sighed. Alayah looked at me with a mix of confusion and surprise.

"Liz being weird? That's unheard of. She's obsessed with you. She loves your guts," she responded, chewing.

"Yeah, I think it's just this whole virus thing," I sighed again, "She's just been...I don't know."

"Well, you're like, the cutest couple so I'm pretty sure it'll be fine," she said positively as she grabbed another slice, "Soon as all this is over, you need to hurry and get married because I'm ready for my godchild." I chuckled a little, raising my eyebrows.

"She doesn't want kids," I told her, and her jaw dropped so far down I could see the chewed up food in her mouth.

"What!?" She exclaimed, "What do you mean!?"

"Exactly what I said," I laughed again. Alayah looked like her entire world had gone down the drain.

"That's not fair! I wanna see little Liz-Luca's running around! And I wanna spoil them with sugar when you're not looking!" She went on. I was amused by her concern.

"You would do something like that," I said back, and she grinned a little.

"I know I would. And I planned to. Now what?" She said.

"She said she didn't want to risk them having my condition, so she said she just doesn't want kids at all," I explained, and her smile turned upside down.

"That's kinda rude, but okay," she mumbled, "Then again, she still hasn't cared to learn ASL for you so I mean, I guess."

"Alayah," I said, giving her a look.

27

"I'm just saying," she said before I could say anything else.

She was right. Up to this point, Liz had no interest in learning sign language. She claimed it was too hard and she couldn't grasp it, so she gave up pretty early on and refused to pick it back up. I let it go because I still had access to my hearing aids, so it didn't seem like a big deal to me. But as much as Alayah liked Liz, that was one thing she hated about her.

"You shouldn't have told me that because now I'm mad," she said, trying to force a laugh to lighten the mood, but I could tell that really upset her.

"Lay, its fine," I assured her, "I understand where she's coming from."

"I'm glad you do because I don't. I feel like that's a really shallow thing to say, but I digress. It's none of my business," she said, then quickly changed the subject as she grabbed a breadstick, "Wow, this is good."

"Alayah," I said again, feeling like I needed to calm her down more, but she grabbed the pizza box and the breadsticks and sat on the floor in the living room.

"Let's watch a movie," she suggested, ignoring me. I couldn't help but laugh again. I guess it was nice to have a friend who was so concerned. Alayah had always been sort of overprotective in that way when it came to me and my hearing disorder. Like this one time in middle school,

This kid, Josh, had been making fun of me all school year. I never showed how much it bothered me, but Alayah knew. It was a Friday, and our teacher always had "fun Fridays" where we wouldn't do any real work. We would play games or watch a movie, but this particular day, we were setting up for "the quiet game". Whoever slipped up

28

and talked or made a noise first would be out. The last one still quiet was the winner.

"This game isn't fair," Josh talked aloud, "Luca wins every time. Everything's quiet for him already!" Almost all the other kids laughed with him.

"Josh!" Ms. Barr yelled at him, "That's inappropriate! You apologize to Luca right now!"

"If I do, can he hear me? He's like an old man," Josh mumbled, causing another chorus of laughter from our classmates. Alayah was seething in her seat next to me. I could see it all over her face. I shook my head at her, already knowing she was going to say something. I was never a confrontational person, so I would never stand up for myself. But you could count on Alayah to do it for me.

Before Ms. Barr could yell at Josh again, Alayah quickly popped up from her chair and smacked his head in between both her hands, specifically hitting his ears so hard that they turned bright red. The smack was so loud, the whole class stood still, including me.

"OW!" Josh screeched.

"WHO CAN'T HEAR NOW, YOU STUPID IDIOT!?" Alayah screamed at him, "Stop making fun of my friend!"

"Alayah!" Ms. Barr snapped at her, surprised she would do anything like that. Alayah was far from a problem child. In fact, she was a teacher's pet, if anything. I mean, I knew she could be loud and strong willed, but she never acted that way in school.

"He started it! He's always being mean to Luca!" Alayah shouted back, stomping her foot down.

"I will handle it, Alayah. Please sit down," Ms. Barr said to her, in a more calm tone, giving her a pass. Then she turned to Josh, "Go to the principal's office.

Now." He stood up, angry and embarrassed, and left out of the room. Ms. Barr had suggested a different game, and the rest of our classmates started talking and laughing amongst themselves again.

I glanced over at Alayah, who was sitting back in her seat. Her expression was still upset until she looked back at me, then she smiled menacingly and cracked her knuckles.

"I bet he won't mess with you again," she whispered, and it made me laugh.

"You know she's gonna tell your mom you did that," I said back to her.

"And I don't care. It was for good reason," she said, unbothered by the possible threat. I laughed again, glancing up to make sure Ms. Barr wasn't watching us.

Alayah had been that way since even before that. She couldn't stand if someone treated me differently, she'd be more upset than me. Honestly, it was kind of funny, but I was beyond grateful to have a friend like her.

Chapter 5: Alayah

Over the next couple of weeks, Cameron and I were smashing like rabbits. I didn't know if he was trying to make up for the trash sex the last time or what, but I was being flipped and folded like a pretzel almost every day, whether it was at his place or mine. He even stayed the night with me a few times just to get more in the morning.

Somehow, though, I still wasn't quite satisfied with him. Not that the sex wasn't good, because it absolutely was and always had been, but it was the aftercare that was lacking. There was no cuddling or talking or anything of the sort. He just dove back into his phone, ignoring me almost until he was ready for another round. Made me feel like a piece of meat.

Now granted, I know being on your phone is a given in this day in age, but I specifically remembered a time when we first started dating where he told me he didn't want to be on his phone while he was with me, because he didn't want anything distracting him from spending time with me. But now, five years later, that sweet logic was out the window, like spending time with me wasn't a big deal anymore.

Other than the occasional double dates with Luca and Liz, we barely went out anymore even before this virus swept through. I was starting to feel like sex was *all* he wanted. I was setting double reminders on my phone each day just to make sure I was taking my birth control on time —even DoorDashed a Plan B over once.

Maybe it was just me, but I was getting the feeling that our relationship was more like a comfort thing than an actual meaningful partnership. And this isolation was making it worse. But, I still loved him, and I didn't necessarily want to end things. I don't know. I felt conflicted.

I didn't want to talk to Luca about it anymore because I knew what he would say. Talking to Cameron about it never helped. He would either just brush me off and tell me I was tripping, or he would get mad and accuse me of wanting to see other people. Just like he had this day.

"Cam?" I said to him, but he didn't answer. Too busy scrolling. "Cameron?" I said again.

"What, Layah?" He said, still not looking up.

"Can we do something?" I asked. He quickly put his phone down on my bed and leaned over, kissing me.

"What do you want me to do?" He asked, but I pushed him away.

"That's not what I meant," I said to him. He sighed.

"What do you wanna do?" He asked, irritated, "We can't go anywhere. And I'm tired of watching movies." I rolled my eyes and put my pink sweatshirt back on.

"We can do other things," I told him, "We can talk. We can play a game. We can go for a walk. Drive around, I don't know."

"I'm not wasting gas to 'drive around', Layah. I still have to get to work," he said back, picking his phone up again. I took it out of his hand and locked it, setting it face down, but he snatched it back.

"Really?" I said to him, disappointed but not surprised. He didn't say anything. "Do you even like me anymore? Or just my cooch?" I asked him after a second. He looked at me like the question surprised him, then he laughed.

"What kind of question is that?" He said, "Of course, I still like you. I love you. That super-soaked cat of your is just a plus."

I cringed. What kinda gross, corny name was that??? The response didn't make me feel better at all. I sighed, the point I was trying to get across clearly flew over his head.

"Why do we always have this conversation all the time?" He asked me, "You don't wanna be with me anymore or something? You bored with me?"

"That's the question I'm asking you! Are you bored with me? All you wanna do is crack my legs open," I said back, standing up and placing my hands on my hips.

"But you like it," he said with a smirk. I literally smacked myself in the face.

"Never mind, Cameron," I said, throwing on a pair of sweatpants.

"Oh, Alayah, come on. I hate when you do this," he said, "Are you being forreal?" I just looked at him. He sighed and shook his head. He stood up and put his clothes back on, too.

"Let me know when you're done acting crazy," he said, collecting his phone and heading out towards the door. I didn't even bother trying to stop him.

Crazy? He thought that was me acting crazy? In what world? I walked out into the living room to grab my favorite throw blanket, then walked down the hallway to Luca's.

"Knock, knock," I texted him, like I usually did. It didn't take him long to open the door.

"Hey, stranger," he joked, "Haven't seen you in a while."

"Please, don't," I said back to him, walking right in. Cameron and I had been tangled in each other so much the last couple weeks, I hardly had time to hang out with Luca. At least I knew he wasn't upset about it.

"What happened now?" Luca asked me, shutting the door.

"Nothing," I said to him, making myself comfortable on the couch, "How are you?"

"Lay," he simply said, following me over and sitting next to me. He knew I was lying.

"Nothing, Luca. I don't wanna keep bothering you with it," I told him honestly.

"You could never bother me," he told me, "and it's not like I have anything better to do." I appreciated him, but I didn't feel like talking about it myself.

"Nothing happened," I lied again, wrapping my blanket around my arms and laying my head on his shoulder. He put his head on top of mine for a moment and laughed a little.

"Whatever you say," he said.

Chapter 6: Luca

After Liz's initial fourteen-day quarantine, she added another whole week just to be safe. I was happy to see her, but she seemed off. I chucked it up to her still lagging from being sick, maybe, and still tried to enjoy the night with her. Even though we couldn't go anywhere, I still wanted to do something with her other than sitting in her room. So, I took her to the park and planned a small picnic since it was Saturday and the weather was nice. *Then*, we went back to hanging out at her house for the rest of the day. I kept trying to keep conversations going with her, but she still seemed so…not herself. And by the time she walked with me back to my car, she was full on sad-faced.

"What's wrong, Lizzie? Are you okay?" I asked her as we stood in front of her parents's house. Somehow, me asking her that only made her become more sad. Her pale blue eyes squinted a little as she reached up to touch my face.

"I wanna talk to you about something, Luca," she said back. She took her hand down and ran her hand through her dark, straight hair and took a deep breath.

"What is it?" I asked her confused by her depressing expression. She paced around the porch and sniffled a little.

"I don't think I wanna get married, Luca," she finally said. I have no idea what my expression looked like, I just knew I was thrown for a loop. What the heck happened in three weeks that would make her say that?

"I don't understand?" I said back to her, "Did I do something wrong?" I grabbed her hand, but she pulled it away.

"No, it's not you," she said, "I'm just having second thoughts, I guess. And… I wasn't really sick." I stared at her, completely lost and still not following where this was coming from, and also a little upset that she would fake being ill—especially realizing she was acting out coughing sprees just for razzle dazzle.

"I just told you I was sick because I didn't…I didn't want to see you until I figured out how to say this," she spoke again, "I don't wanna get married this young. I love you, I really do. I still wanna be with you. I just don't wanna get married. Not right now." She slid the ring off her hand and placed it in my palm.

"Liz, I don't get it. If you felt this way, why wouldn't you just talk to me? And why would you wait all day, after we've been together to say anything?" I asked her, trying not to sound as upset as I was. I felt completely blindsided.

"I just wanted to enjoy the day with you, I guess. Because I knew you'd be mad at me for saying this," she said, looking at me. I was at a loss for words. She stepped closer to me and wrapped her arms around me, but I couldn't bring myself to hug her back. She kissed my cheek.

"I still wanna be with you," she said again, "Just not as a fiancée. Being your girlfriend was fine enough."

"Why didn't you just say that when I asked you then?" I questioned.

"Cause you were so sweet and you put so much effort into it and I didn't want to ruin it. I didn't want to say no in front of my parents and my friends. I figured maybe the idea would grow on me, but it hasn't," she explained.

"I'm sorry," she said after I had no response, then went back inside the house. I think I stood there for a while, still trying to figure out what just happened.

*****

I sat on the couch in silence, wracking my brain trying to think back on what could have possibly led Liz to such a decision, but I couldn't think of anything.

Alayah knocked on my door. I told her to come over so I could tell her what happened, and she was there in seconds flat. I opened the door for her and she came bopping in, happy per usual until she saw my somber expression.

"What's wrong?" She asked me, her eyebrows pulling together in concern.

She pushed her clear glasses up her nose and tied her thick, curly hair up as if she was gearing up to hear whatever I would say next. I held up Liz's engagement ring in my hand and Alayna's jaw dropped.

"What happened!?" She shouted, closing the door behind her as she stepped further inside.

"I wish I knew," I sighed, tossing the jewelry across the room. I ran through what happened to her, sitting on the couch again. Saying everything out loud didn't help either, it made it seem even more ridiculous.

"Okay, is it bad I kinda wanna fight her? Cause what the heck? Why would she do this to you? You literally love her so much," Alayah rambled, just as perplexed as I was, "What the heck?"

"I mean, I noticed she started acting weird shortly after I gave her the ring, but I didn't think it was because she wanted to say no," I thought out loud after another big sigh.

"Well, of course not. She took the ring and said yes. If she was gonna be a weirdo, she should've said something a long time ago!" Alayah said, walking back and forth around the couch with her hands on her hips. I agreed with her on that. She shook her head and sat next to me.

"I'm sorry, Luca," she said, then asked confused, "Are you still together or was that it?"

"I think so?" I replied, "She said she didn't want to break up, she just doesn't wanna marry me." Alayah's eyebrows pulled together again, visibly unsettled.

"I don't see how that makes sense, but okay," she said after a while, "What about how you feel, though? Do you still wanna be with her? After that?" I just shrugged.

"I don't know. I still care about her, but what's the point now?" I thought out loud again.

"Don't worry about it, buddy," she said after a while, and placed a comforting hand on my shoulder, "I'm still here."

"I'm not sure that's any better," I joked back, my mood lightening just a little bit.

"Rude!" She laughed and playfully punched my arm. Then, it was quiet for a minute.

"We should do something," she suggested after a while.

"Lay, it's after eleven. Everything is closed," I said back.

"Well, let's take a walk or something," she proposed, "Being closed in these four walls isn't gonna help your crying."

"Who said I was crying? I'm not crying," I laughed out loud.

"Exactly, let's keep it that way," she said, standing up. I laughed again as she pulled me up by my arm. We stopped by her apartment so she could grab her shoes and a jacket, then we took the elevator down to the main floor of the building and went outside.

We strolled down the sidewalk for a while, the streets were dead being that it was late at night. It was starting to rain, just a light sprinkle, but with the warmth of the May air, it wasn't a bother.

A few cars drove by, their tires splashing up rain water as they passed. Traffic lights and street lights were the only thing illuminating our view. Most buildings were dark and still. We walked until we came across the gas station a few blocks down. It was still lit up and busy. Surprised that they were still open, we went inside and roamed around for a little. We hadn't planned to actually go anywhere, so we didn't have any face masks that we were required to wear in any establishment, but the employee working didn't say anything.

"Hey, look," Alayah whispered to me, motioning towards a slightly older couple standing at the check out counter. I laughed a little, knowing exactly where she was going with this. One of the weird things we always did was make up stories about the random strangers we saw at any given time, coming up with outlandish backstories just for a laugh.

"She's probably making him buy one of those sex pills," she signed to me, and I couldn't help but laugh out loud. Alayah covered her mouth, trying not to laugh as loud as I did.

"They're way too old for that," I signed back. She made a face at me.

"Exactly. She's fed up about him not being able to stand straight any more," she signed, and it kicked off another round of laughter.

"What if it's her getting the pill? She might be battling the Grand Canyon right now," I signed, and Alayah laughed so hard, she was squealing.

"Okay, game over. Shut up," she signed and said out loud, walking around the aisles to the candy section. I followed her, laughing.

We grabbed a bunch of snacks and two giant slushee fountain cups. After we checked out, we walked back to the apartment building and hung out in her place, which was far more decorated and put together than mine was.

There was a dark green loveseat couch against the window wall with a plush rug in front and a matching swivel chair next to it. On the other side of the couch was a small table with a lamp. Her tv sat on a tall stand with shelves and cabinet doors. In the corner across from there was her work station, a small desk with a computer, a landline phone, and scattered sticky notes and pens. Her kitchen area was the same size as mine was, but somehow hers looked bigger with how cozy she had it decorated with pictures and candles and string lights.

She kicked her shoes off and sat in the swivel chair, immediately cracking open a bag of gummy worms from the store. I reclined comfortably on the couch and turned the tv on like I lived there. I might as well have. The way she and I were always back and forth between our two apartments, it might have been cheaper just to be roommates.

We sat around and talked for a while until we passed out right there in the living room. I appreciated her distracting me from what happened with Liz. One thing about Alayah, I always knew I could count on her to be there if I needed her. And I made sure I did the same for her. Through past breakups and whatever else, we always got each other through it. Like the first time I ever got dumped.

Sophomore year in high school, I dated Emily Thompson. She was in our art class, and always sat with me and Alayah, and this other kid at the square desk we usually sat at towards the back of the room.

Emily was blonde and very pretty. I didn't think she liked me until she started passing me notes in class. She thought I was cute, and she was into me because I could draw, and even asked me to sketch her face a couple times. Alayah encouraged me to go for it, she was like a proud sister so excited for me to have my first girlfriend.

Emily and I dated almost the whole school year. She came to all of my baseball games, I walked her to all her classes, we hung out after school. I thought it was going great, until she just simply decided she was over it and wanted to date someone else. Now it seemed silly, but back then I was heartbroken. But Alayah was there, saying the same thing she said to me that day:

"Don't worry about it, buddy," she said, sitting with me out on the porch, "They'll be other girls who'll let you sneak through their window when their parents aren't home." I laughed out loud.

"That was one time," I said back.

"Well, whatever. You couldn't stop smiling for days," she teased me, grimacing like she was disgusted.

"Shut up," I nudged her, still laughing.

"Ha, got you to smile. I won," she smirked, "Come on, lover boy, let's go to the store and get some candy. It'll make you feel better." She stood up and started down the sidewalk. I followed behind her, amused by her constant humorous nature.

We had been friends for years, ever since I could remember really. Her mom and mine were really good friends since childhood, so it was a given that we would be around each other a lot. But as we got older, we weren't just friends because our parents were. We were friends because we actually had fun together and could trust each other with anything. She was the closest friend I had.

Chapter 7: Alayah

I could not wrap my head around Liz calling off the engagement with Luca. Like, was she insane? Luca was the sweetest person I had ever known. And he was attractive, with his dark brown eyes and shaggy, dirty-blonde hair that kind of curled at the ends. He was athletic and tall. He had a decent paying job and had plans for them. And he wouldn't hurt a fly! I was confused. Why wouldn't she want to marry him? It didn't make sense.

As for my own headache, Cameron, I hadn't seen him in a week or two after our last conversation, and you know what? Thank goodness. My brain and my body needed a break from him anyway. He barely texted me, which was odd for someone who was constantly on his phone. But, whatever. He'd come around eventually. He always did.

One day, as I focused on work, my computer went down again. So, I meandered down the hall until I got to Luca's door once again and knocked without texting first. But, he answered without too much waiting.

"You're lucky I was already standing by the door," he signed to me.

"Shouldn't you have your aid in while you're working?" I signed back.

"I'll use it when I'm needed," he signed with a laugh, "What is it now?"

"My computer again and the WiFi."

"I think your break that thing on purpose just to see my face," he signed, and laughed at me. I nudged him.

"Shut up and fix it, please," I signed back, laughing too. He closed his door behind him and followed me back to my apartment. I sat in my wheelie chair and gave him space to look at whatever this machine was doing now. He clicked around with the mouse and attempted his IT magic, but nothing was happening.

"We might be here a while," he signed after a long time.

I groaned out loud, and picked up my landline phone for work. I dialed my supervisor and told her what was going on. She gave me permission to use my personal laptop to finish out the day and excused me from taking any work calls because of the technical issues. Fine with me. I hated taking calls.

Luca tried his best but he was just no match for the beast of the computer. So he quit, and we both went back to his apartment. I carried my laptop in my arms into his bedroom where his workstation was set up to mooch off the WiFi. He sat at his space and logged back into his software, and I sat on the bed crisscrossed with my laptop in my lap.

But of course, we couldn't just let each other work in peace. What kind of boring day would that be? We ordered pizza again and talked and goofed off the entire time, occasionally being serious whenever he was on the phone.

After the "workday" was over, Luca powered down his computer and I was way too happy to shut my laptop. I noticed the sketch book sitting on his dresser and grabbed it. I flipped through it, looking at the intricate and realistic drawings.

"Tell me why you're not doing something with this," I said to him, still flipping through. He glanced over at me to see what I was talking about and laughed a little.

"Like what?" He asked, turning around in his office chair.

"I don't know. You could be a tattoo artist. Or work in an animation studio. Or draw comics for the newspaper, I don't know. Something," I said back. Luca had always loved to draw. In fact, he used to get in trouble in school for sketching and not paying attention while the teachers were up talking. I remembered how he used to draw sketches of the girls he would date in high school, and they would fall hard for him every time. But I mean, could you blame them? If someone took time out of their day to draw a flawless sketch of my face, I'd probably fall hard, too.

"Nobody reads the newspaper anymore, Lay," he replied, standing up.

"You know what I mean," I rolled my eyes at him and handed him the book, "Shouldn't let such a talent go to waste."

He laughed again, setting it back down on the dresser, then he walked out to the living room. Opposite from me, Luca was never the type to want to be in any type of spot light. He was perfectly content keeping his hobbies and secret talents to himself.

"Can you draw me?" I asked him, following him out.

"I could," he shrugged, turning the tv on.

"Now?" I asked with hopeful eyes, "And I'll hang it on the fridge like a proud mom." Once again, he laughed at me.

"Sure, Lay," he said. He went back to grab the sketch book and a pencil box of various pens, pencils, colored pencils, markers and sharpies. He sat next to me on the couch and faced me.

"Are you ready?"

Chapter 8: Luca

"You can't move, so pick a spot and stay there," I laughed as Alayah fidgeted next to me.

"What if my head itches?" She asked.

"You gotta suffer," I teased her, and she threw her head back.

"Ugh, fine," she said, and repositioned herself on the couch to face me. She ran her hands over her hair and took her glasses off, but I shook my head.

"No, keep them on," I told her.

"Why?" She exclaimed.

"Cause they're literally apart of your face," I joked some more, "Whenever I think about you, I think of you in your glasses. They gotta stay on."

"Aw, you think about me?" She joked in a sing-song voice and smiled obnoxiously big.

"Put your glasses on, Alayah, and hold still," I laughed. She laughed, too, and straightened up again. I put my pencil to the paper but she stopped me.

"Wait! Should I smile?" She asked. I dropped my face in my hands and chuckled.

"Alayah, please. Stop moving," I said to her.

"Sorry! Okay, okay," she giggled. She pulled herself together again and smiled a little, only exposing the top row of her teeth. Finally, I started.

Sketchbook in my lap, I glanced back and forth between her and the paper, doing my best to capture her. The room was quiet other than the faint hum of the refrigerator, but I could barely hear that either as I dove into a deep concentration.

I glanced up at her again out of habit really. I probably could've drawn her from memory better but since she was right here, I made sure I got everything right. Her long curly hair cascaded over her shoulders, framing her face in a way that made me pause for a second. Her big brown eyes looked back at me, contrasting her almond-colored skin in the most perfect way. I did my best to capture the likeness of the curve of her lips and graceful lines of her jaw and cheekbones on the paper. Her soft smile grew bigger as she laughed at herself, struggling to stay still.

Alayah had always been beautiful. That wasn't a secret, but I don't think I had ever taken the time to look at her this closely before. At least not lately. And now, as I studied her face to draw it, a different kind of admiration started to creep in my mind. But I shook it off quickly.

"My cheeks hurt," she laughed through her teeth, and it snapped me out of my daze, "I shouldn't have smiled. Bad idea."

"Relax your face," I chuckled, "I'm done with that part for now." She sighed dramatically and relaxed her whole body.

"Can I see?" She asked, leaning over to look, but snatched the book from my lap and held it close to me.

"No," I laughed, "I said I was done with that part, not completely done. Sit back." She slouched back in her seat, pretending to be annoyed, but I could tell she was just excited for the outcome.

She watched me intently as I finished up, adding some color and small details. When I was finally done though, I hesitated for a second. I didn't know if I wanted her to see it just yet. I held the book against my chest, almost hiding it.

"Let me see!" Alayah said, but I shook my head.

"I lied, it's not done yet," I said to her.

"Luca! I wanna see it!" She protested, laughing a little.

"It's not good enough. I might have to do it again," I replied. That a was normal feeling I always had after drawing anything. The second guessing. The doubting. Probably why it was something I just did as a hobby and not seriously.

"Lucaaaa," she whined. She slid closer to me and reached for the book. I closed it and held it up over our heads where she couldn't reach it.

"No, I changed my mind," I said back, stubbornly.

She started laughing and just about climbed on my lap to stretch her arm up as far as she could. I moved the book behind my head, making it harder for her to grab, turning it into a frustrating but hilarious game as we argued back and forth.

She reached behind me a little further, but the combined weight of both of us leaning caused the futon to flip over. We flew backwards, tumbling onto the ground and the sketchbook shot out of my hand, sliding across the hardwood.

Alayah landed right on top of me, both of us in a hysterical laughter and tangled up on the floor. She laughed so hard, she could barely lift her head up from my chest. When she finally looked at me, she had tears in her eyes from laughing and it made everything even more funny.

Finally, she got up and searched for the sketchbook that landed in the kitchen area. She picked it up and flipped through until she got to herself. I stood up and fixed the couch, and walked over to her. A smile spread across her face and her eyes lit up as she looked at the picture, then she looked at me.

"I like this!" She said excitedly, "Looks just like me. Why didn't you wanna show me? It's perfect."

"I don't know. I'm weird," I shrugged.

"Sign it for me," she suggested, holding it out to me, "So when you're famous, I can tell people I have an autograph on one of the first masterpieces you ever drew." I chuckled as she shuffled back over to the living room to grab a pen from my collection of writing tools.

"Sign it," she said to me again. I took the pen from her and wrote my name in cursive at the bottom corner.

"Happy now?" I joked, and she flashed a big grin.

"Yes," she said back. She carefully pulled the picture from the book and held it in her hands. "Come on," she said, then headed for the door. I followed her down the hall and to her apartment.

Alayah stood in front of her refrigerator and moved around photos she had up of her and her family out of the way. Then, she neatly pinned up the drawing with magnets dead center. She stood back and admired it.

"Perfect," she said proudly. She looked up at me, smiling. I looked down at her and laughed a little.

"You're funny," I mumbled, walking back towards the door, "What would I do without you?"

"Die of boredom," she answered quickly with a laugh, walking after me.

Sounds about right. If I didn't have Alayah, especially now, I wouldn't know what to do with myself.

"If our parents weren't friends, I don't think we'd be friends either," I said to Alayah, one day in the summer before senior year of high school.

"Why do you think that?" She asked me, sitting up from laying in the grass in my backyard. I sat next to her, squinting my eyes at the sun.

"Cause you're popular and outgoing and everybody likes you. But I'm not any of that. You're, like, out of my league," I told her. She laughed at me.

"Shut up. We are not just friends because our parents are," she replied, shaking her head.

"No, I know. I just mean, in a different life or something, would we be as close if we met under different circumstances?" I asked. She smiled a little and put her hand on my shoulder.

"Luca, you'd be my best friend in any life. I hope you know that," she said. I remember how good that made me feel, hearing her say that. I smiled back at her.

"We're like two peas in a pod," she continued, laying backwards in the grass again, "Two squirrels in a tree. Two cherries on a stem. Two nuts in a sack."

"Okay, see," I laughed, laying back, too, "You do so well, and then you just don't."

She laughed out loud, the sound of it echoing through the breeze. My friendship with Alayah wasn't just by chance. She genuinely was the best friend I ever had.

Chapter 9: Alayah

A few days later, Luca and I headed to his parents' house. Even though it had been a couple weeks already, he hadn't told them what happened with Liz, yet. He talked to his parents often, but he spent too much time trying to understand the situation and telling them would've meant reliving it all over again. But now that he seemed to be fine with it, here we were going to visit them. And I was the moral support.

We drove over in his car. It wasn't a long drive, they just lived on the other side of town, not too far from my mom's house actually. It was a nice day for once now that the weather was finally turning into spring again. The feeling of sitting in the car without a big, bulky jacket was the best feeling ever.

Luca pulled into the driveway and we got out of the car. We stepped up to the periwinkle colored house with a white front door, but before Luca could knock, his dad, Matt, opened the door. They were already expecting us. He was happy to see us both, it had been a while since we were over there.

I followed Luca into the house where his mom, Amy, was waiting in the living room with a smile on her face. He and I both signed "hi, mom" to her at the same time and it made her laugh a little as she hugged me. She was like a second mom to me; she and my mom were best friends, and I learned just as much from her.

Luca looked like her the most. She had the same dirty-blonde hair, pulled back in a ponytail, the same color eyes and entire face structure almost but with softer features. His dad, on the other hand, had dark hair and green eyes, and was a burly man with a thick beard.

"How are you guys?" Amy signed and spoke at the same time. She was completely deaf at this point, and even though she used hearing aids, too, she still preferred to sign while she spoke for extra clarity. So we did the same.

After some small talk, his dad went to the kitchen to whip up some lunch for all of us while we continued to talk with his mom in the living room.

"How's Elizabeth?" Amy asked. Luca and I both grimaced. "Oh, no. What happened?" She said, reading our expressions.

"She called off the engagement," Luca signed back without his voice, as if saying it out loud would make it sound worse. His mom's jaw dropped.

"What!" She exclaimed, but Luca laughed.

"It's fine," he signed, "It's not a big deal. We're still together. Just not getting married, I guess."

"Matt, come here!" She shouted to the kitchen, and his dad came back. "Liz called off the engagement!" She repeated.

"Thank God," Matt said, "I hated that girl." I laughed out loud. I was not expecting him to say any such thing. His mom sighed.

"Well, yeah. She wasn't the best," Amy responded as she signed, "I guess I have to agree."

"Why didn't you say anything before?" Luca chuckled at their words.

"You seemed like you were sure about her. We didn't wanna get in the way of that," his dad replied, "but we never really liked her for you."

"She could be a ditz, honestly. And she refused to learn sign language," Amy shook her head, thinking back.

"That's what I was thinking!" I exclaimed. Luca glanced over at me, amused but not surprised that I was taking their side on that aspect. His parents went back and forth exposing everything they secretly hated about Liz. I couldn't help but laugh. Luca looked like he wanted to laugh, too, but he didn't. He just patiently waited until they were done ranting.

"We're still together," he said again, since his parents were talking and joking mercilessly like they had broken up.

"Sorry, sorry," his mom said, holding back more laughter, "I'm sorry, I didn't mean all that."

"I did," his dad said, heading back into the kitchen. I covered my mouth, quieting my laugh.

Matt still listed complaints about Liz as he finished up lunch: sandwiches and fries he made on the stove. We all joined him in there and ate, moving our conversation to other things. By the time we left, I think Luca was thoroughly entertained by his parents's true feelings, and so was I.

"We should take shots today," I said to him once we were back in his car.

"What?" He laughed, "Shots for what?"

"I don't know. Your parents's jokes put me in a good mood and I'm bored," I explained, chuckling again.

"Are you not seeing Cameron today?" He asked me, referring back to a conversation we had earlier that day. But, I shook my head.

"I don't really want to see him if I'm being honest," I said to him. Spending time with Cameron only meant two things right now, being used and being ignored. I didn't feel like dealing with either of those things right now.

"Well, I'll definitely take a shot for that. I've never heard you say that before," Luca joked, and I nudged him.

"I didn't say I was leaving him or anything," I said back, "I just don't wanna be bothered with his attitude today."

"That's a step in the right direction to me. I'll take it," Luca continued to tease me, but deep down I knew he wasn't joking.

"Just drive to the store," I said, giving him a light punch to the arm. He laughed at me.

"Vodka or whiskey?" He suggested, raising an eyebrow.

"Definitely vodka," I said back. He laughed again and started the car.

"I knew you were gonna say that," he said as he pulled off.

He drove to the supermarket and led the way straight back to the alcohol section. We looked around for a few minutes before just deciding on our usual preference: New Amsterdam.

It had been a long time we even drank any, though. It wasn't something we took part in very often, just on occasion. So, I thought this was an occasion that called for it. We strolled through the aisles to pick up different kinds of juice for a chaser, and then we headed back home.

Luca followed me into my apartment and we immediately cracked open both bottles we bought. I searched through my cabinets to find our designated shot cups, small glasses with 'best friends' written across them in pink and blue. We got them as a joke after we both turned twenty-one, but I couldn't seem to ever get rid of them. I slid Luca his glass and handed him a bottle.

"Do the honors, my friend," I said to him in an announcer voice, and he carefully poured us both a clear shot. We held up our glasses and counted.

"One," I said.

"Two," he continued.

"Three!" We said at the same time, then threw them back. He and I both made disgusted faces and shuttered at the strong taste, then we laughed at each other.

Chapter 10: Luca

Alayah turned her tv to the YouTube app and started playing music. Then, she went back over to the kitchen area to mix drinks like she was a bartender. She danced and bopped her head to the songs playing as she made random concoctions on the kitchen island with the vodka, cranberry juice, sprite, and various lemonades she picked out at the store. And I was the taste-tester whether it was good or not.

After a while, her many drink mixtures started to take effect on both of us. Whether it was the vodka or Alayah spinning around so much, I was slightly dizzy already. The tipsiness made everything fuzzy like watching a tv with static. The room was a little off-balanced but somehow more vibrant, the music seemed louder, and a nice feeling of carelessness took over.

I could tell Alayah was feeling it, too. Her dance moves seemed to slow down and become more fluid while she used the tv remote as a microphone to keep singing. Her laughter filled the space as she caught herself singing the wrong words, and it made me laugh.

"I think you're done," I said to her from the couch.

"I think *you're* done!" She shouted back, then laughed out loud. She walked over to me and held her hand out. "Dance with me," she said, but I almost couldn't hear her and it wasn't because of my non working ears. I shook my head at her.

"Are you not drunk enough?" She laughed, dropping closer to my face. I laughed again, almost too hard, at the way her eyes crossed trying to focus on me even with her glasses on.

"You know I can't keep up with you, Lay," I said back to her.

"Too bad," she said and signed at the same time. Then, she grabbed my hand and pulled me off the couch.

I couldn't tell you what song was playing or who it was by. She held onto me for balance and I was doing my best not to step on her bare feet. But even though I wasn't much of a dancer like she was, she always made things fun, drunk or not.

After some hours, we had definitely tired ourselves out and the alcohol was starting to have that sleepy effect on both of us. We sat on the couch again, talking about nothing and not even listening to each other but responding anyway with different topics. We laughed at each other's slurred words and losing our train of thought.

Alayah resulted to trying to sign while she spoke, but she was not making any sense even worse and it sent me into hysterics. Then at some point, she switched our glasses to be silly and we couldn't even speak from how much we were giggling.

"I may be deaf, but you're definitely blind," I said to her, squinting to see our of her lenses.

"Not any more blind than you!" She laughed out loud. I took her frames off and put them down, and she did the same with mine.

We laughed and talked more, stumbling over our words. She complained about Cameron, venting that the way he was acting towards her seemed to be getting worse. I couldn't say anything. My answer to her would always be to just break up with him, but I knew she wouldn't listen. She was a beautiful girl who deserved better, but I didn't think she could see that herself just yet.

I ranted about Liz, my drunken thoughts coming out of suppression finally. I didn't understand her. She didn't want to marry me but she still wanted to be with me. She wanted to talk, but barely ever answered when I called or texted her. She said she loved me still, but I hadn't felt that from her in a while, if I was being honest. I wasn't quite sure how her calling off the engagement would affect us, but I knew I didn't like the way I felt ever since she said it. I wasn't sure what to do. Not even the drinks could clear my head to answer that.

******

The next thing I remembered after that was waking up in the morning, loosely wrapped in Alayah's throw blanket on the couch. She wasn't anywhere, I assumed she found her way to her room at some point.

Everything was just as we left it. Empty bottles and juice containers sitting on the kitchen counter without lids, our shot glasses and other random cups we drank out of on the floor. The tv was in sleep mode with the screensaver going. I sat up and immediately felt a pounding headache. I rubbed my eyes for a second and got up to go to the bathroom. Then, I knocked on Alayah's room door even though it was half open.

"Are you alive?" I asked her through the door.

"Are you?" She asked back, and I chuckled a little.

"No," I answered.

"Same," she said, "You can come in." I walked all the way into her room where she was laying at the foot of her bed, half under the blanket.

"Come," she said, scooting over and patting the space next to her. I casually laid beside her and faced her. "This was a mistake," she continued, slamming her face into her pillow.

"It was your idea," I laughed.

"Well, stop listening to me all the time," she replied, laughing, too. I grabbed one of her pillows and hit her with it. She grabbed another one and hit me back.

"I don't even have the energy for this," she said after a second, "Help."

"I feel just as terrible as you do," I said back after a yawn.

"Ughhhhh," she mumbled, burying her face into a pillow again and I laughed at her. "We're never doing that again," she said.

Chapter 11: Alayah

Luca continued to laugh at me as I took the pillow away from my face. I sat up, rubbing my eyes and stretched. I sighed, my head absolutely booming from however many drinks I had. Luca noticed my wild mess of hair and pulled out a piece of lint tangled in my curls, flicking it to the floor with a smirk.

"Yikes," he said, his voice still a bit groggy.

"Shut up," I said back, nudging him, and he laughed at me once again. He had such a prince-charming type of smile. It could've just been the remaining haze from the alcohol, but he looked really cute even as he laughed at my misery. Liz was a total idiot.

He got up and walked back out to the living room, and I followed. We cleaned up the disheveled area quickly, Luca throwing away all the empty bottles and me wiping down counters, sticky from spilled drinks. I washed out the shot glasses and put them away, and he straightened out the couch cushions and folded my throw blanket neatly.

"I'm gonna go take a shower," Luca said after the room was decent again. He picked up our eye glasses from the floor and handed me mine.

"Are you coming back?" I asked him, and he looked at me like I should've already known the answer.

"Don't I always? I don't have any other friends but you," he said back with a shrug. I laughed a little.

"You have other friends, Luca," I reminded him.

"Not any I hang out with every day. You're my favorite by default," he said jokingly. I placed a hand over my heart dramatically.

"Aw, I'm so gonna remember you said that," I replied, "You're my favorite, too."

"What was that?" He said, turning his ear to me. I knew he was messing around and just wanted me to say it again. I rolled my eyes.

"You're my favorite, too," I repeated. He literally took his hearing aid out and turned it off, backing up towards the door.

"What?" He shouted, and I laughed out loud.

"I'm not saying it again!" I shouted back, signing. He chuckled, very amused by his own shenanigans, then left out.

I walked back to my bedroom, preparing to hop in the shower myself. The stream from the hot water made my lingering headache ease up a bit. I washed and brushed all the tangles out of my hair and leisurely lathered my body. The steady flow of the shower head ran down my skin, rinsing the fun chaos of the night before down the drain.

*****

Later that day, Luca and I sat on my couch again flipping through the channels when one of the news stations caught our attention. A newscaster reporting on the pandemic virus per usual and going over the new statistics of the casualties it caused since it started. Seeing the crazy numbers added to my anxiety about it.

"Looks like I won't be going anywhere," I said out loud.

"We don't go anywhere as it is," Luca responded with a laugh, changing the channel.

"Well, now I'm really not leaving," I said back, adjusting my sitting position so that my legs were crisscrossed, "Walmart grocery delivery and DoorDash it is from here on out. Anybody that wants to see me can only get as close as a FaceTime call. Maybe. Travel pack of Lysol spray in my pocket at all times." Luca laughed a little.

"I think we'll be okay," he said, glancing over at me.

"I know we will because we're not going anywhere," I reiterated, and he laughed again.

"Not even for your boy?" Luca asked me, teasingly. I rolled my eyes at him.

"There may be an exception there," I admitted, "But then again, he doesn't get to work from home like I do. He might catch something and then I'm at risk. So maybe not."

"Well, according to old sci-fi movies, we're on borrowed time. The end of the world is near," he chuckled, "So to be safe, I'd tell him to stay away from here, too."

"You're just saying that because you hate him," I laughed. It felt like I reminded us both about that fact way too often.

"No, I'm saying that because I don't wanna be sick," he said back.

"Oh, like Liz and her fake hacking?" I joked back, then faked a cough to be funny. He glanced over at me.

"That's not funny," he said, but I could tell he wanted to laugh. Leave it to Luca and I to go back and forth, making fun of each other's relationships. He flipped through the channels some more before handing me the remote to pick something to watch.

"Do you really think it's the end of the world?" I asked him after a moment, and he shook his head.

"No, not hardly," he said, "I think it's just a series of unfortunate circumstances like all other crazy diseases throughout history. Like the Spanish flu and the bubonic plague and Ebola and swine flu and whatever else. These things just happen every so often. Like clockwork." I smiled a little, trying not to laugh.

"You're such a nerd," I joked. He looked over at me again, grabbed a couch pillow and threw it at me. "Can you stop doing that?" I laughed out loud.

"Nope," he simply said, tossing another pillow at my face.

I laughed again, grabbing both pillows and throwing them back at him. The banter escalated into a full blown pillow battle, cushions flying everywhere while we laughed and screamed at each other. At this point in life, I'm sure our surrounding neighbors just learned to accept our loud existence. There was never a quiet day when we were hanging out together.

My mind went back to a random day when we were probably about eleven or twelve years old, sitting in his parents's living room. A bowl filled with a mix of popcorn

67

and M&Ms between us on the couch and the tv playing
cartoons, we were tossing the snacks back and forth trying
to catch the pieces in our mouths as a game and keeping
score.

"That's four for me," Luca said after a successful
catch.

"Lame," I said back, and he laughed. He reached
in the bowl again, and leaned backwards.

"Okay, your turn," he said, one eye closed to see
for perfect aim. I set myself up, ready for my attempt, but
when he opened his hand, several M&Ms hit me dead in the
face. Luca laughed hysterically, nearly rolling off the
couch.

"You didn't catch a single one of those!" He
shouted in his laughter.

"Why'd you do that!?" I laughed, too, throwing a
pillow at him. He threw another one back, and it turned
into a silly fight, just like now. We were having so much fun
and laughing so loud, Luca's parents weren't even mad we
almost destroyed their living room as we launched pillows
across the room at each other. That is, until one of the
cushions hit his mom's porcelain flower vase and shattered
it.

Luca and I both stopped in our tracks, jaws dropped
and frozen. Amy stared us, hands on her hips and an
expression on her face that absolutely said we were in
trouble.

"Sorry, mom," He and I both said to her at the
same time. Her face softened into a smile, and she shook
her head.

"Clean it up," she told us, nicely. Luca grabbed the
broom and I grabbed the dust pan, carefully picking up the
pieces as we continued to laugh.

Chapter 12: Luca

A couple weeks went by and Liz still refused to come over. And now that the rising cases of the virus were skyrocketing, she didn't want me coming over at all either. The only connection I had to her was calling her in the morning and before I went to sleep (if she even answered) and texting her throughout the day. It was starting to feel like she didn't want to talk to me at all, honestly, but I didn't want to think like that. I think she thought I was mad at her for calling the engagement off, but I wasn't mad. I just didn't understand, but I let her have it because I didn't want to lose her. But whatever this was now, it felt like I was already losing her regardless.

Alayah hadn't seen Cameron in a while either. Any time he asked to come over, she would tell him no. Even though she denied it to me, I think she was finally starting to be fed up with him. But still, she wouldn't leave him. I think we both found some sort of solace in each other and hanging out more was a good distraction from both our relationships.

After an attempt to pull an all-nighter just for fun one Friday night, she and I both passed out on her couch at some point. When I opened my eyes, it was bright outside and whatever we had been watching on tv was long over. Her curls lightly brushed against my face, and I realized she was wrapped around me pretty tightly. I gently smoothed her hair down away from my nose, and she shifted a little, squeezing me closer to her like a stuffed animal.

I slowly pulled my phone from my pocket to see that it was 11am. The last time I checked, it was four in the morning and I didn't remember falling asleep at all. I didn't want to wake her up or move her, she seemed so comfortable. And I guess, I was, too. Was that weird? She shifted again a few minutes later and slowly lifted her head up to look at me.

"Did we make it?" She asked me, sleepily.

"I don't think so," I said back, shaking my head slightly.

"Ugh," she sighed, laying her head back on my chest, "So close. We gotta try it again. I wanted to see the sunrise."

"I'm not doing that again," I laughed, "That was way too hard. I'm surprised we made it as long as we did."

She giggled a little, but then when she realized our position, she sat up quickly. She fidgeted with her hair, smoothing it over and trying to shake off the sleepiness. I sat up after her, slower, almost wishing she hadn't moved just yet. I wiped off my glasses with the bottom of my t-shirt, glancing at her. I felt like I wanted to say something, but I didn't know what. We had fallen asleep on the couch countless times before, but this time was a little different. I didn't think it was a bad thing. Was it?

"I'm hungry. Are you hungry? I'm hungry," she said, popping up from the couch and walking over to the kitchen. I chuckled.

"Lay—" I started, but she cut me off.

"Don't make it weird, Luca," she said, turning around to look through the fridge. I laughed again, putting my glasses back on my face, but I think it was more of a nervous laugh. Then, I walked to the kitchen, too. She closed the fridge and stood on her toes to reach the box of Frosted Flakes cereal on top of it. I reached over her head and grabbed it down for her.

"Thanks," she said, taking it from me. It was awkwardly silent for a long time.

She opened the overhead cabinets to grab a bowl, then back into the refrigerator for the milk. She took a spoon from the utensil drawer, and leaned against the counter to eat. I walked back over to the couch. The awkwardness in the room lingered for a while, but soon was forgotten when her phone rang.

"Hi, mom," she answered it, then put it on speaker while she made another bowl of cereal.

"Just checking on you, making sure you're okay," her mom said back. Their voices sounded just alike.

"I literally haven't left these four walls," Alayah told her, "So I'm good. Are you good?"

"Absolutely. I'm not going out in the craziness," her mom said, then added, "Hi, Luca!" I laughed at her automatically knowing we were together.

"Hi, mom," I said back. She was just as much a second mom to me as my mom was to Alayah. They continued to talk, mostly just conversing about what was going on in the news. After a while, I got up to leave.

As I walked down the hall back to my apartment, I called Liz. For some reason, an odd feeling washed over me, almost like guilt, and I just wanted to talk to her. It rang and rang and rang. Straight to voicemail. I sighed, walking through the door. I went to my room and laid backwards on my bed. I stared at the ceiling, my train of thought wandering…

Chapter 13: Alayah

Talking on the phone with my mom did not distract me from the matter at hand. It was weird. Luca and I were friends. How the heck did we get huddled up like that anyway? I didn't even remember falling asleep to begin with! Maybe I was overreacting. Maybe it wasn't as weird as I was making it. I mean, we had fallen asleep on the couch before, but not like that. Luca thought it was funny. He didn't seem phased. So why was it so weird for me? After I hung up with my mom, Cameron texted me as if on cue.

"I miss you I wanna see you, Layah" the message said. I rolled my eyes.

At this point, it had been weeks since I saw him. It was probably just the new restrictions causing a sense of urgency, but he had been texting and calling more. Then again, he always seemed to act better if I began to fall back, which I had been doing lately. Not just because of the virus, but I just didn't want to deal with being ignored. I had nonsexual needs that weren't being met. I didn't want to just act like animals on sight every single time we saw each other. I wanted to talk, I wanted to have fun, I wanted to lay up and cuddle, I— oh.

I hoped the way Luca and I woke up wasn't my fault. I had been so deprived of Cameron's nonexistent love for so long that I could've cuddled up to Luca in substitution, subconsciously in my sleep.

I felt so cringey towards myself. I hoped he wouldn't tell Liz. She probably wouldn't think it was funny like he did, and I didn't want her to feel some type of way towards me. Because for a moment a couple years ago, she had suspicions that there was something going on between him and I with the way we constantly hung out together. But when she realized that wasn't true, she just accepted our close friendship. I didn't want those suspicions coming back, because that's absolutely not a thing.

Now that I thought about it, I hoped that wasn't the reason she gave the ring back. Maybe she felt like we were spending too much time together again because of the lockdown, maybe her suspicions were already back.

I put my face in my hands. I was stressing myself out. I took a deep breath to relax. The whole sleeping on the couch was throwing me into a spiral. I texted Cameron back.

"Miss you too," I sent, but I wasn't sure if I missed him at all.

"Let me come over," he texted back. When I didn't answer right away, he FaceTimed me. I answered.

"Baby girl, I wanna see you," he said immediately when his face popped up on my screen, "If you don't want me to come over there, just come here."

"Uh, no," I said back, "Have you not been watching the news?"

"Ugh, Layah, come on. I'm not sick," he said.

"That you know of. You could be a carrier," I told him, raising my eyebrows matter-of-factly.

"See, this is why I told you to just move in with me before. I knew you were gonna be weird," he replied.

I thought back to March when all this first started. He had suggested that I live with him so we wouldn't be dealing with all this back and forth now, but I genuinely didn't want to do that. He and I had been on and off for far too long for me to give up my own place and live with him. If we broke up again, then what? Then I'd have no where to go. Absolutely not.

"Your apartment is basic, Cam," I said, making an excuse, "I don't wanna live there."

"Then let me move in there," he suggested, but I quickly shook my head.

"Oh, gosh, no," I laughed, "For you to man-ify my cute, cozy living space. Nope."

"You're full of it, Alayah," he said back, and I couldn't help but laugh again. He was not amused.

"I'm being real," I responded, finally standing up from the couch to walk into my room.

"Being real lame," he said back, a hint of irritation in his voice, "I wanna see you, bro." He always called me 'bro' when he was getting mad. I think he thought it upset me but I thought it was funny.

"You wanna see me or you wanna sex me? Because those are two different things," I mumbled, but he heard me anyway.

"Well, you're not letting me do either so what do you want me to do?" He said back, his voice raising a little. Oh yeah, he was definitely getting agitated. I really didn't have an answer for him. I sighed.

"Cam, this isn't just a cold or a sore throat or something. It's serious. I don't think we should be back and forth like that," I finally said after a second.

"Okay, Layah. Bye," he said, and without any further delay, he hung up. Did we just break up? I wasn't sure. But for some reason, I was laughing. I walked back out of my room and down the hall.

"Knock, knock," I texted Luca. I was fine until he opened the door, then seeing him reminded me of the couch again. The awkwardness came back with a vengeance.

"Hi," I said, laughing again, this time awkwardly.

"Are you alright now?" He asked me, amused by my laughter.

"I think," I said, walking inside. Then, I continued, "I just got off FaceTime with Cam and I don't know what just happened." Luca looked at me confused. I sat on the floor in the living room and told him about the conversation and Cameron's abrupt end to it, all while still giggling.

"Why are you laughing?" He asked, sitting across from me, "Call him back and ask for some clarification."

"I'm not calling that man back," I chuckled, "It's whatever. I don't care."

"Yes, you do. I think you've actually lost your mind this time," Luca joked, "You've finally cracked." I laughed more, and I still didn't know why. Whether it was the awkwardness I still felt from the morning or just finally fed up with my boyfriend, I don't know. But, I was hysterical.

"Did you talk to Liz?" I asked after I finally calmed down.

"No, she wouldn't answer," he shook his head.

"Were you gonna tell her?" The question was eating at me. Luca looked at me, perplexed.

"Why would I do that?" He asked me, and I just shrugged. "Like you've never fallen asleep on my shoulder before," he said with a laugh, "It's not a big deal." I appreciated the downplay, but still, the other thought I had weighed on me.

"What's wrong, Lay?" He asked me, reading my expression.

"You don't think Liz thinks we're being too close again, do you? And that's why she's being weird?" I said to him. He thought for a second, then shook his head.

"I doubt that," he said, "I don't know why she's being weird, but I'm sure that's not it. She understands why you and I are so close."

"Are you sure? Cause I can talk to her," I suggested, my concern rising. Luca smiled a little.

"You don't have to do that, Lay," he told me, then he looked to the floor, "At this point, whatever happens happens."

"Luca," I said to him, feeling a little sad for him, "you wanted to *marry* her."

"Thanks for reminding me," he said sarcastically.

"No, I just mean, that's a big thing. You don't have to pretend like you're not upset just to keep the peace with her. I think you should talk to her, like really talk to her," I told him.

"She doesn't answer," He said, finally looking up, "I can't talk to her if she doesn't answer. And if I told her how upset I actually was, I know she would..." he trailed off, taking his glasses off and rubbing his eyes stressfully.

"I don't even know if I'm allowed to be upset," he continued, "If she doesn't want to take the next step, then who am I to tell her she can't feel that way?"

"You're allowed to be upset, Luca," I said back, "Same way she's allowed to feel whatever she's feeling. I personally think she's wrong, but I am biased. She should be *running* to the alter to marry you. I would." He looked up at me again, and smiled a little.

"That came out wrong," I quickly added, my eyes widening realizing what I just said, and he laughed.

"You wanna marry me? Not Cameron?" He teased. Slightly embarrassed by my slip up, I put my face in my hands and laughed awkwardly.

"Actually," I said, looking up again, "If we're not married by the time we're forty, I think we should just go for it." Luca chuckled and nodded his head.

"Might as well," he shrugged, still smiling a little. My nervous laugh came back, and I looked down at the floor.

"You are biased," he said to me, after a while, "Same way I'm biased when it comes to you." I rolled my eyes thinking about his disdain for Cameron. Maybe Luca *was* right about him this whole time, though. It just took a massive, world isolation for me to see it.

I remembered the first time I met Cameron. We were college, third year students, and he was in my psychology class. I'm pretty sure I checked him out first, as he sat two rows in front of me. Chocolate brown skin, neatly twisted dreadlocks, and a bright white smile—I could almost see the cartoonish sparkle glisten every time he smiled. I wanted to talk to him, but I didn't know how to break the ice. So after class, I walked near his seat and dropped my textbook on purpose.

"Ugh," I scoffed, using my acting skills to seem really annoyed. I started to reach down to grab it, but Cameron beat me to it. He scooped my book up, along with a few papers that scattered across the floor.

"Have you always been in this class?" He asked as he handed my stuff back to me, with this sort of smirk on his face.

"Yeah, I have," I told him, smiling back.

"Nah," he shook his head, "I would've noticed a gorgeous girl like you in here." I laughed at him. He was so corny, but so fine to me.

He was a football player, and I was on the dance team. It was like we fit so well, like a movie. He would buy me flowers, take me on cute dates, romantic as all get out. Seemed like he couldn't get enough of me. Now, it was hard to believe there was a time he actually cared enough. But, the hook he still had on my heart was deep enough that I went back every time he messed up. Ugh. Maybe I was the idiot.

Chapter 14: Luca

The more Alayah and I bonded over the strange turn our relationships were headed in, the less upset I was. Alayah had a way of making the most unfunny things absolutely hilarious. She had a thing for dry humor. I think it helped her feel better, too. According to her, she hadn't heard from Cameron in a long time. I probably talked to Liz, once, maybe twice a day, and the conversations were dry. I just let her have her space. I felt like I needed it, too.

So, Alayah and I just filled the space, keeping each other entertained and distracted as time moved into August. She hung upside down in her swivel chair, laughing at the episode of *Catfish* that was on. It was one of our favorite shows to watch together. We had been watching it for hours, and it was almost one in the morning.

"I'm sleepy," I said to her, listening to her chuckle.

"Wait, no! One more episode! Don't tap out yet, " she said back, sitting up straight.

"Alayah, please, I'm so tired. And you know I will absolutely stay and watch another episode," I laughed. I stood up and stretched, and walked to the kitchen. She followed me.

"I wanna catfish someone," She joked, and I laughed out loud.

"Shut up," I said. "Don't do that. Why would you do that?"

"I don't know. It might be fun," she laughed, too.

"I'll tell on you," I told her, "I'll call in that day and expose you."

"Wow! Where's the loyalty?" She laughed again. I opened the refrigerator to take out a container of juice, and got us both cups from the cabinet.

"Love how you act like you live here," she said, amused.

"You do the same thing at my place," I reminded her, "Did you forget?"

"This isn't about me," she laughed, nudging me. She picked up the cup I poured for her and sipped out of it at the same time I drank out of mine.

"You're really gonna leave right at *Catfish* peak?" She asked after a second.

"Lay, it's 1:03am. I'm not pulling another all nighter with you," I chuckled a little, "I'm going to bed."

"You're no fun," she rolled her eyes jokingly. I laughed again, finishing my juice. I washed my cup out and put it back, then told her I'd see her tomorrow, of course.

I walked down the hall to my apartment, the rest of the building was quiet. Just the hum of the ceiling lights buzzing. As I walked through my door, I thought about the day with Alayah. She always tried so hard to make me feel better about Liz, but she didn't know that I nearly forgot about Liz whenever I was with her. But as soon as the day was over, then I'd think about her again. I thought about dialing her, but I didn't want to feel the disappointment of a unanswered call again.

The quiet of my apartment mirrored the silence of the hallway, and I felt a pang of loneliness for a moment. I put my phone down on the counter, debating on if I should call one more time, or if I should just let it go. She was probably asleep now anyway, it wouldn't make a difference if I did or didn't. I sighed, and walked right back down the hallway, knocking on Alayah's door.

"Did you miss me already? It's been like eight minutes," she teased me, opening the door. I laughed a little.

"I'm sleeping on the couch," I told her as she let me in. I guess I didn't really want to be alone at that moment.

"Okay," she said, not needing any further explanation, "Happy to have ya." She passed me her throw blanket and the tv remote, then went to her room.

"Goodnight," she said before closing her door half way.

"Goodnight," I echoed her. Then, I turned out the lights in the living room and settled on the couch, the tv the only thing still on. Knowing that Alayah was close by while my thoughts were still spinning made things a little easier.

*****

"What are we doing?" I asked Liz the next day. I only sent a text. Surprisingly, she replied pretty quickly.

"What do you mean?" Her message said.

83

"??? Why won't you answer me?" I asked.

"I've been busy with school," she said back. I didn't want to go back and forth over messages, so once again, I called. No answer.

"You're not serious," I texted her again. Those three little dots popped up as she typed, then disappeared for a moment.

"I'm busy," she said again.

"I wanna talk to you. We're still together, aren't we?" I replied.

"Yeah," her message plainly said.

"We haven't really talked in weeks Lizzie."

"I know. Sorry. I'll call later, I promise. Just not right now."

"I love you."

No reply.

I sighed and turned my phone over face down on my desk. I had to get back to work, I couldn't stress about that right now. I wasn't sure what her deal was, but this was affecting me than I wanted it to. I guess I would just continue to give her space. That was the only thing I could do. Saying we were still together was one thing, but not talking to me was something different. The signals were mixed and I was definitely confused, but I didn't know what else to do.

Chapter 15: Alayah

My conversations with Cameron were getting shorter, but my days with Luca were getting longer. Our tight-knit bond was getting even closer, and I'd be lying if I said I didn't like it. And between me and my own mind, there was something about Luca that was catching me all of sudden. I wasn't sure what it was, but there was something.

He and I lounged on the floor in his apartment several days later in an intense game of Uno. He leaned backwards on his side, propped up on his elbow and hiding his stack of cards in his right hand. I was across from him, lying on my stomach with my last cards fanned out in front of my face. We took our turns laying our cards down, occasionally exchanging mischievous glances.

"Uno," I said, laying my second to last card down. Luca raised an eyebrow at me, his expression full of playful challenge and a permanent smirk. Was it weird that he was cute to me? I always knew he was a handsome guy, but now it was different. I giggled a little, meeting his eyes. I had been giggling the entire time.

"Why are you laughing so much?" He asked me, laying down a card, completely unaware of the internal battle I was having.

I think it was just the isolation, but he was becoming more attractive to me every day. I thought back to the other day when we woke up on the couch together. I wished I hadn't been so awkward about it. It wasn't *so* bad. But then again, it was weird, right? Such an out of place thing to happen, regardless of how much time we were spending together. We had spent time together our entire lives and it never felt like this. Well, maybe once or twice.

When we were teenagers, there was a brief moment when I had a tiny, minor crush on him, but I knew he never thought of me that way. So, I ignored it. Now, it was probably just the lack of communication from the outside world that had me misplaced. Luca and I were friends. Just friends.

"I win," I simply said back, letting my last card float down to the scrambled stack of cards on the floor, then said again, "Uno." Luca shook his head, still with a smirk. He had just lost for the third time in a row.

"I let you win," he said to me, sitting up.

"You did not," I said back, laughing. I sat up and tucked my legs under me.

"I want a rematch," he laughed.

"No, we've played like seven times already," I reminded him, collecting the cards from the floor.

"Well, let's make it an even eight," he said.

"No," I laughed, "You're mad you lost." He laughed again, then glanced to the floor at my phone buzzing violently.

"Cameron's calling you," he said, his smile fading a little.

"I don't care," I said back. I ignored the call and flipped my phone face down.

The more Cameron called and texted me, the less I wanted to respond, which lead to unsolicited nudes from him—and again, only made me *not* want to respond. I'm not sure why he thought sex was the answer. It wasn't. He was still my boyfriend, but this break from him was way too enjoyable to be normal. Luca wondered why I wouldn't just break up with him, but I still loved Cameron. I just wasn't sure if I was *in* love anymore. And I needed more time to think about it.

"Are you finally done?" Luca asked me. I was tired of him asking me that. He knew the answer, he just liked to be a jerk about it.

"Are you?" I asked back, then faked a cough to refer back to when Liz pretended to be sick. Luca laughed out loud.

"Just play me again," he said, holding out his hand for the cards. I handed them to him and our hands grazed each other's for a split second—which wasn't an abnormal thing, but it felt weird. I looked up at him, wondering if he noticed, but his expression remained unchanged as he focused on shuffling the deck of cards. I exhaled, louder and sharper than I intended to, shaking off whatever I thought was happening.

"We don't have to play again if you don't want to," Luca laughed, probably thinking my haste was towards him.

"No, I wasn't being snappy," I chuckled. "Let's go sit outside or something," I suggested, as if the fresh air would clear my clouded brain.

"Okay," he agreed, and shoved the UNO cards back in their box. We put our shoes on and went to go sit outside on the fire escape stairs outside of the window.

The August breeze was warm and whipped my hair around wildly. I tied it back with the scrunchie from my wrist. It was really a shame the pandemic had just about everything closed down. We could've had more fun going places like summers in the past, but this was life until further notice.

We sat next to each other on the narrow, metal stairs, watching the quiet streets below. I looked up at him, seeing if his face triggered the same feeling outside of the apartment that it did inside of it. If that even made sense. He looked back at me, his eyes questioning but amused at the same time.

"What?" He asked. I turned away and took a breath to say something, but then I just laughed.

"Nothing," I said back, "I'm just going insane, I think."

"Yeah, same," he said, but I knew for a sure we couldn't have been talking about the same thing. I glanced at him again to see him still staring at me, but with a different expression I couldn't quite place. We weren't talking about the same thing, right?

Right?

Chapter 16: Luca

    A few of Alayah's curls escaped from her ponytail and floated in the breeze as she laughed. I rested my chin in the palm of my hand, watching her. I most definitely was going crazy, too, but not because of isolation like she was referring to. Being in constant proximity of her was confusing me lately.

    I mean, there were a selective few times years ago, when we were teenagers, that I thought maybe we could have been more than friends. Having someone who understood me so well at such a young age had definitely piqued my interest in her several times. But then, the idea seemed so far-fetched as the years went by. *But now*, that feeling seemed to be circling back. And every time I looked at her, I felt guilty knowing that Liz and I were still technically together. But Liz never called me that day like she promised. I didn't know what we were doing.

"Do you remember the other day when we were talking about the end of the world?" Alayah asked me after a while.

"That was weeks ago, but yeah," I chuckled a little.

"What if this really was it?" She said, and I laughed more.

"It's not," I said, "it's no where near apocalyptic enough."

"Oh, what, like your video games?" She joked, and I glared at her for a second. "What if it was?" She asked again.

"Then you'd have to be stuck with someone who's ears don't even work," I teased her.

"Luca!" She exclaimed, like she was horrified I'd ever find humor in my disability, "Don't say that."

"Okay, but seriously. What good would I really be in an apocalypse? The batteries in my hearing aids only last a couple weeks at a time. After that, then what? I'd be dead cause I wouldn't be able to hear the zombies coming after us," I replied, cracking up at the thought.

"I don't like when you do that," she said back, "Stop making fun of yourself."

"It's not that serious. It doesn't bother me," I told her, still laughing a little.

"Well, it's serious to me. I hate when you do that," she said, looking at me, "And I wouldn't call it being 'stuck'. But for lack of a better word, being *stuck* with you isn't a bad thing. I'd rather it be you than anyone else."

I smiled a little, glancing back at her. She smiled back just for a second. And for that split second, I thought maybe we might have been on the same page, but then she looked away.

"Besides," she added as she stood up, "If the zombies come for us, I'd probably die, too. You can't hear, and neither of us can see. I'm not a fast runner. We're doomed either way." I cracked up laughing again.

"So I can't make fun of myself, but you can?" I asked her, and she nodded.

"Exactly," she teased, crawling back through the window to get inside. I followed her. She sat crisscrossed on the couch, and I sat beside her.

"Chinese for dinner?" She suggested, but I shook my head.

"No, I want tacos," I said back.

"We literally had tacos two days ago," she groaned, then stood her ground, "Chinese or nothing." I raised an eyebrow at her and a grin spread across her face. Thinking the same thing, we immediately engaged in a Rock-Paper-Scissors fight. I won, my Paper covering her Rock.

"Ha!" I shouted.

"Ugh, not fair!" She laughed, "Best two out of three."

"No! I won," I said pulling out my phone to open the DoorDash app, but she reached for it, starting another hilarious fight.

"I don't want that!" She laughed, just about wrestling me for my phone.

"You're gonna flip the couch again," I teased, dodging her. She sat back down, remembering when it happened.

"Well, I'm getting Chinese anyway so, ha," she said back, matter-of-factly, taking her phone out, too. I laughed at her.

"You're not offending me. I don't care," I joked back. She covered her face, laughing hysterically.

Being "stuck" with anybody else definitely wouldn't have been as entertaining as being with Alayah. Even as I thought about what it would've been like to be paired with Liz during the lockdown instead of Alayah, it definitely wouldn't have been the same. Regardless of whatever I was feeling, I couldn't deny that.

Chapter 17: Alayah

"Suspect is nowhere to be found. But it's quiet. Too quiet," I spoke into a toy walkie-talkie as I crouched behind my swivel chair, "Suspect lost the last round, though, so I'm not worried."

"I *can* hear you, you know," Luca's voice said from the bathroom. I laughed out loud.

"You were supposed to!" I said back. I peeked from behind the chair, watching him slowly walk out of the bathroom with a blue Nerf-gun in his hand. I ducked back down as close to the floor as I could get, pointed my orange Nerf-gun at him and fired three foam darts that bounced off his chest.

"Ha! Gotcha!" I sprung up from the floor triumphantly.

"You have three seconds," he said back to me with a smirk. I quickly collected my darts from in front of his feet, then ran out of the door. His footsteps ran after me down the hallway. I laughed, reloading, and dashed into his apartment. I ran into his room and hid in the corner behind his workspace.

"Alayah?" He said menacingly, "Where are you?" I tried to stay quiet, but my laughter gave me away. He stood in the doorway, looking dead at me but I jumped up, dodging his shot.

"Ha-ha," I teased, sticking my tongue out like a little kid. He shot at me again, but I spy-rolled across his bed and landed on the floor on my feet. He laughed at me, almost hysterically.

"What is wrong with you?" He joked.

"I'm winning by five successful shots," I told him, standing up. Then, I pointed my Nerf-gun at him again, "You're slacking." Before I could shoot, he ducked out of the doorway. I ran after him, and we chased each other around the room going in circles and missing shots.

We ran back out into the hallway, laughing and giggling like we were twelve years old. I chased him down the narrow corridor, but he was too fast for me and hopped into the elevator. He waved goodbye teasingly as the door shut before I could catch him. I laughed and sprinted back down the hall to the stairs, hoping to beat him to the first floor. But my legs were way shorter than his, I wasn't sure if I would make it.

My lungs were on fire as I just about jumped down the stairs, my footsteps echoing in the empty stairwell. I don't think I had ran so much in years. When I reached the lobby of the building, the elevator doors were just opening. Luca looked surprised and entertained that I actually caught up. We aimed our toy weapons at each other and fired, successfully hitting each other.

"That was really fun," I laughed, out of breath. Luca picked up the foam darts from the floor and tucked them in his pocket of his sweatpants. He smiled at me, catching his breath.

"Yeah, I feel like I'm gonna pass out, though," he said.

"Same," I exhaled sharply, "We're taking the elevator back up." He chuckled a little and pressed the button for the elevator.

We stood next to each other, shoulder to shoulder as it took us back up to the third floor. I looked up at him, his hair a tad bit shaggier than usual from sweating, but it didn't take away from his attractiveness at all. The confined space of the elevator seemed to amplify the moment. Luca looked back at me, sticking his tongue out like I had done to him earlier to make me laugh. I giggled a little and looked away.

I started to feel that feeling again. That weird, warm feeling that I felt whenever I looked at him now all of a sudden. It was like a gentle flutter of excitement and nerves, which was odd. The first time I noticed was the day after we partook in all that drinking, but I wasn't drunk right now. For a split second, I wondered if it was mutual, if he felt that shift when he looked at me, too. I rolled my eyes to myself. There was no way he did. He was still in love with Liz, regardless of whatever they were going through, and I knew that. I shook off whatever I was feeling just as the elevator stopped.

The elevator dinged, and my moment of insanity was broken as the silver doors slid open to let us out. We walked back to his apartment and threw ourselves on the floor, to continue to relax from the vigorous battle we had.

"I'm hungry now," Luca said after a while.

"Please, do not say tacos again. I will literally die," I stressed, and he laughed at me.

"Actually I was gonna say we should make pasta because the spaghetti sauce in the cabinet is calling my name," he said back, and it made me laugh out loud.

"Calling your name?" I repeated, laughing hard.

"I said what I said," he laughed, too. Then, he stood up and walked to the kitchen area.

"You're funny," I replied, sitting up from the floor.

"Come help me," he said, but his tone wasn't goofy anymore, more like he was asking in an endearing way. A way that made me smile and jump up to walk over to him. I found a tall pot from the cabinets and filled it with water to boil the noodles in, while Luca retrieved all the ingredients from the pantry.

"Okay, wait," I said, pausing for a second, "We can't do this without music." I skipped back over to the tv to turn on the YouTube app again, so we could have some background tunes while we cooked. Luca glanced at me, already knowing I was about to pull out my dance moves like I always did.

I swayed and twirled around the kitchen area, purposely bumping into Luca to annoy him. He laughed at me, occasionally glancing at me in amusement while the ground beef browned on the stove. As the water started to boil, I added the noodles in and a pinch of salt, stirring them around with a wooden spoon as they softened. Our eyes burned as we chopped onions and green peppers to add to the meat sauce.

"Why are you crying?" I teased him, laughing. He laughed, too, rubbing his watery eyes.

"Why are *you* crying?" He joked back, wiping an onion-induced tear from my cheek. His touch on my face made me giggle and shy away. I couldn't tell if it was the vegetables still or wishful thinking that he winked at me, but my stomach flipped.

As the sauce simmered, Luca and I tossed single noodles on the wall, waiting for them to stick to test if they were done or not, almost making a game out of it. I placed the strainer in the sink and he carried the pot over, carefully letting the noodles fall into it.

From the tv, Maroon 5's "This Love" played and I ran over to turn the volume up even louder. It was one of our favorite songs, and we belted out the lyrics word for word, using the cooking spoons as microphones, drum sticks, and guitars. We ended up playing it six more times while the food cooled down. Laughing and singing around the entire room together did nothing to help the shift I kept feeling, it only made it worse.

Instead of sitting in the living room to eat, we just stood over the counter, hunched over our plates side by side.

"This is the best spaghetti we've ever made," I said after a while, "We outdid ourselves." Luca nodded in agreement and glanced at me.

"See, my dinner ideas are good," he said back jokingly. I giggled a little, noticing a small drop of red sauce on his chin.

"You got a little something on your face," I told him.

"Well, don't just stare at it. Where is it?" He said back. I giggled again and leaned a little closer to him, and swiped it away with my thumb.

"Am I good now?" He asked, making a bunch of silly faces and wiggling his eyebrows.

"What face is that?" I laughed.

"My sexy face, of course," he joked, and I cracked up loudly. "Don't you like it?"

"Oh, swoon," I said sarcastically, "Such a ladykiller." He chuckled and nudged me. Ugh, that smile was ruining me so bad. I almost wanted him to stop laughing. What was happening?

Chapter 18: Luca

      I convinced Alayah to watch a horror movie with me after we ate. She usually hated them, but we had already watched way too many comedies and sci-fi films so far. She was wrapped in her favorite throw blanket on the couch, claiming she was cold but it was really for moral support. She sat with her knees hugged to her chest, prepared for any jump scares that might come, but we were only a few minutes into the movie.

      "Are you gonna be okay?" I teased, laughing at the contrast between her in survival mode and me next to her, casually lounging with the popcorn bowl in my arm. I got up to turn out a few lights for a better effect, then sat back down.

"Of course," she said, trying to sound nonchalant, "If you get scared, though, I'll protect you." I laughed out loud.

"Yeah, okay," I said wryly with a smirk.

The eerie soundtrack of the movie filled the room and shadows flicked across the walls as the scenes changed. Alayah pulled her blanket closer under her chin and sunk backwards. I slid a little closer to her, and she slightly leaned into me, her blanket still tightly gripped in her fists. We sat close a billion times, but at that moment, my nerves tensed up. I glanced at her, half amused by her stance, but also making sure she wasn't too afraid. If it was too much for her, I'd turn it off.

Without thinking though, I left her at some point to go to the bathroom. I wasn't gone long at all, but I knew I missed something by the expression on her face as she stared at the screen.

"Are you scared?" I asked, sitting next to her again. She screamed and jumped so hard, she kicked the popcorn bowl up in the air. Popcorn rained down from the ceiling and the hard plastic bowl crashed to the floor. I couldn't help but laugh.

"Why did you do that?!" She shouted at me, followed by a smack to my arm.

"I promise I wasn't trying to scare you," I said to her, almost doubled over in laughter. I grabbed the remote and paused the movie, but she glared at me. Even though I was laughing, I felt really bad.

"I'm sorry, Lay," I told her.

"No, you're not," she said back, hitting me again.

"Alayah, I promise I didn't mean to," I said again. She glanced at me again, trying to be mad, but a smile crossed her face.

"I hate you," she signed in ASL, her voice quiet.

"Are you not gonna talk to me now?" I chuckled, and she shook her head. "I'm sorry," I signed back.

Her smile widened a little, though she tried to hide it. Then, she turned her attention towards the tv again, unpausing the film. The glow of the screen complimented her face as her expression softened. She didn't seem too shaken anymore, after directing all her energy at being mad at me for scaring her.

I wasn't too interested in the movie anymore, though. I stared at her, watching the way her eyes widened slightly at some creepy scenes, how she bit her lip in anticipation, and the occasional laugh after realizing the effects weren't as scary as she thought.

My mind wandered, trying to figure out what was different. What was it that was making me care for her just a little bit more than usual? I hoped I wasn't too obvious, but I could not take my eyes away from her. It was messing me up. I scratched through my hair, confused that I couldn't place what was happening. She finally looked over at me, and her eyebrows pulled together noticing the confusion on my face.

"Are you okay?" She asked me. I straightened up quickly and forced a laugh.

"Yeah," I said back, "Are you? You forgive me now?" She smiled softly, and she flicked a stray piece of popcorn from my shirt.

"I guess so," she replied.

******

Later that night, there was a bad thunderstorm and it knocked the power out in the whole building. The crash and whirring of electricity powering down woke me out of my sleep even without my hearing aid. I couldn't see right in front of me. I grabbed my phone from under my pillow for light, it was two in the morning. I texted Alayah and asked if she was okay. I knew she hated storms, and after the scary movie earlier, I was sure she was freaking out. She immediately replied.

"I'm coming over," her message said.

"I'll meet you half way," I sent back. I put in my aid so I could hear since I couldn't see and walked out into the hallway, using my phone's flashlight. Alayah came out of her door at the same time, her phone flashlight flickering around as she shuffled over to me in her pajamas.

"All of days, why today?" She whispered angrily, and it made me laugh. She reached out for my arm for guidance and followed me back into my apartment.

"You can have my room, I'll sleep on the couch," I told her.

"Are you sure?" She asked, shining her flashlight upwards to illuminate our faces. I squinted from the bright light.

"Yeah, I don't care," I assured her. She bumped into me slightly as she walked back towards my room, leaving the door half open.

The storm continued for a while, rain pelting down on the roof and windows, thunder and lightning cracking and rumbling loudly. It was almost impossible trying to go back to sleep.

"Luca?" Alayah called.

"Yeah?" I answered.

"It's too dark," she said, and I laughed a little at her stating the obvious.

"Are you okay?" I asked her again.

"No, come back," she replied. I chuckled again, and made my way to her in the dark. "I can't even see you," she giggled quietly, hearing my steps come in.

"I can't see you either," I laughed.

There was no light, not even a stray streetlight from outside to peek through the blinds. The bed slightly creaked as she made room for me to climb in next to her. The more my eyes adjusted, I could just barely make out her silhouette as she faced me. Even though I couldn't really see her, my heart raced a little, feeling her presence so close to me. Despite the sounds of the storm, there was a stillness that was somehow comforting. Although, this wasn't the first time we shared a bed.

It was years ago, we were probably fifteen or sixteen years old. Alayah's mom, Stacia, worked at a hospital at the time and one particular day, she had to work an overnight shift. She didn't want to leave Alayah at home by herself so she stayed at my house. It thunder-stormed that night, too.

Alayah was supposed to sleep in the guest room, but she and I were in my room talking for most of the night. She watched me play my video games while she talked about things that happened at school that week. Soon as the thunder and lightning cracked, she wouldn't leave. Of course, I didn't mind. I let her have my bed and I set up a little blanket pile on the floor. Another round of thunder and lightning sounded, and she leaned over the bed.

"Luca?" She whispered loudly.

"What, scaredy-cat?" I laughed at her.

"Come up here. Cause I am scared," she laughed, too.

"Lay, you're fine. I'm right here," I told her,
looking up at her. Her long curls hung down past her face
as she leaned down more.

"No, you're there. You're not here," she continued
in a whisper-yell. I chuckled again.

"Alright, fine. Move over," I replied. I got under the
blanket next to her and we faced each other just how we
were now. I remembered she grabbed my hand, although I
was sure it wasn't a big deal to her. But to me, it triggered
something. And I wanted to kiss her.

That was exactly how I was feeling now. I
wondered if she remembered that. I wasn't going to ask her,
but then I decided to.

"I forgot about that," she laughed a little after I
recounted the memory to her, "I guess nothing has changed.
You were a lifesaver then and you're a lifesaver now. I hate
bad storms."

"Always a scaredy-cat," I said back. She laughed
again quietly.

"Shut up," she nudged me.

"You shut up. Go to sleep," I joked, nudged her
back. She giggled as she snuggled the blanket up to her
chin. She closed her eyes, but I couldn't stop thinking about
the parallel between that old memory and now.

Within minutes, I could hear her soft snore and
steady breathing. Knowing that she was okay now and
comfortable enough to rest, I finally closed my eyes, too. I
almost wished the power would never come back on just to
make this moment last a little bit longer.

Chapter 19: Alayah

The sun softly filtered through the blinds and curtains in the morning, clear the storm had long passed. I woke up, almost forgetting where I was until my eyes focused on Luca on the other side of the bed. There was a good bit of distance between us, but still I felt close to him. It was making me nervous for some reason, and I felt the need to fix my hair and make sure I didn't have any gross eye crust before he woke up. Luca's eyes gradually opened after a moment, and he looked at me.

"Hi," he said to me after a yawn.

"Hi," I said back with a shy wave, noticing his hearing aid resting on the pillow beside him.

"How did you sleep?" He signed.

"Good," I signed back. Maybe this wasn't as weird as I was making it seem? I mean, he didn't seem phased. My nerves held me back from asking, which was odd in itself because I was never nervous to talk to Luca about anything. Except for now.

He got up after a moment and stretched, then walked over to the light switch and flicked it on and off a few times. It didn't seem like the electricity wasn't back on, yet. Luca shrugged and continued to the bathroom. I sat up and grabbed my phone that was about to die. No power meant no work—fine with me. I could use a free day.

"What do you wanna do?" Luca signed to me when he came back. I thought for a second.

"I don't know," I signed back with a shrug.

"We can go to my parents' house until the power comes back on. Or we can go somewhere else," he suggested, standing in the doorway. I weighed the options in my head. Going anywhere else seemed like a chore. At this point I was so used to not going anywhere, that actually leaving seemed strange. He grabbed his aid, put it in his ear, and turned it on. Then, he grabbed his glasses from his work desk and put them on his face.

"Your parents' house is fine. I might walk over and check on my mom, too, while we're there," I signed back.

"Go get dressed then, scaredy cat!" He shouted exaggeratedly, and it made me laugh. I walked over to him, nudging him as I passed.

"Don't act like you didn't like it," I teased back, but really, I was testing his reaction.

"I didn't say I didn't," he chuckled a little, "Best sleep I ever had." His response made the butterflies come back and I tried to hide my smile, but I still wasn't quite sure if he was serious or still just joking around.

****

Luca dropped me off at my mom's house that was only a block away from his parents's place. I figured I'd stop by there first, then walk over back to him later on.

My mom and I small talked for a little, there wasn't much to talk or gossip about when the whole world was in quarantine. I charged my phone and told her about the power getting knocked out and spending the rest of the night at Luca's, but I did *not* tell her that we shared the bed. Regardless of knowing the whole story, she smirked at me as she lounged back on the sofa. She stirred her tea cup and took a sip, then sat it gently on the small table beside the couch.

"When are you just gonna date that boy?" She asked me, and I laughed out loud nervously.

"Why would you say that?" I asked her, "We're just friends, mom. You know that."

"Pfft," she rolled her eyes, "No one said it had to stay that way."

"Please!" I laughed again.

Unfortunately, my mom was just like me. Or I was just like her, I guess. Very bubbly and excited over the silliest ideas, and this one was one of them. Her idea of Luca and I ending up together was on her mind since we were kids. She wasn't the only one who teased the possibility either. Over the years, our old friends did, too. But my friendship with Luca was so strong and important to me, I couldn't think about ever ruining it—even with these new feelings that were developing in me right now. The idea was absolutely absurd, actually. Wasn't it?

"I'm just saying," my mom said with a shrug.

"You're just saying because that's your best friend's son," I said jokingly.

"No, I'm saying that because I'm tired of hearing you cry over boys who don't even care about you, Alayah," she said genuinely, then she smirked again, "But, Luca? Luca definitely cares about you." Once again, I laughed out loud.

"In what world?" I asked her, leaning back and crossing my legs, prepared to hear her argument.

"Alayah, it's obvious. It's always been obvious," she said. She grabbed her tea cup and took another few sips, then stood up. "And that's all I'm saying about it," she added, then walked into the kitchen.

"How is it obvious?" I asked following her, "He's still with Liz."

"Is he? I thought Amy said that girl called off the engagement?" my mom said quickly, rinsing out her cup in the sink.

"She did but they're still together," I informed her, but after I said it, it was like it was brand new information to me, too.

I thought about last night and this morning. How strangely good it felt to be close to Luca, but that fact was still technically true. He was still in a relationship with Liz. And I thought I still with Cameron, even though I hadn't seen him in a while. Boy, was I confused.

"Well, I didn't know that. If she gave the ring back, the relationship should've been over, but that's not my business, I guess," my mom said, not noticing my internal struggle at the moment. Sounded just like I had, though. Calling off an engagement seemed like break up words to me, but I wouldn't know.

"Yeah, so you're wrong," I said to her, still in my own head. My mom made a face as she turned off the sink water, then nodded to herself.

"Okay, I hear you," she simply said, but there was a hint of sarcasm in her voice. I sighed. She changed the subject soon after, and I was absentmindedly responding as she spoke, still way too deep in my own thoughts.

Chapter 20: Luca

"Can I talk to you about something?" I asked my mom, almost immediately when she opened the door for me.

"Yeah, what's wrong?" She signed as she spoke. I followed her inside and we settled in the kitchen. It was just us in the house, my dad was still at work. He did not have the luxury of being able to work from home like my mom and I did.

I leaned over the counter island in the middle of the floor and sighed. I tried to get my thoughts together before I said anything, but I couldn't form a coherent thought to even start with.

"I'm confused," I finally said.

"About what, Luke?" She asked with a concerned look in her eyes.

"Alayah," I replied, and sighed again. Her eyebrows raised a little, then she tucked her lips in, trying not to smile.

"What about Alayah?" She probed for more details.

"I don't know," I covered my face for a second, stressed in my thoughts, "I feel like things are different, but I don't know if it's just me. Or if it's the lockdown. Or if she…I don't know. But I look at her, and I just…I don't know."

My mom was quiet for a second, watching me scramble for words that I didn't have, but somehow she understood exactly what I was trying to say. She smiled a little more genuinely and looked at me.

"Why don't you just tell her?" She asked.

"I can't," I said quickly, "What about Liz?"

"What *about* Liz?" She echoed me. I looked at her even more confused.

"She's still my…girlfriend," I told her, and she made a face.

"You hesitated," she said back. I dropped my head and put my face in my hands again.

"Okay that's the point I'm making," I sighed, then started rambling, "I don't know what to do. Liz keeps saying we're still together but she barely talks to me or lets me see her. Alayah's still with Cameron but she would rather just hang out with me than him. He's stupid anyway, he never treated her right. I feel like she might feel the same way I do, but I actually have no idea. And if she doesn't, then it's gonna make everything weird and ruin everything and I don't want that."

"That might be a risk worth taking. Because what if she does?" She said back, but it didn't make me feel better. Actually, it made me feel nauseous, and it shouldn't have. I was twenty-five years old, having feelings for someone wasn't anything new to me, but this just felt so different.

"I've seen the guys she's dated before. I'm not even her type," I said after a while. My mom chuckled.

"Is that what you're telling yourself?" She asked, amused, but I didn't find it funny. "You've loved Alayah your whole life. Your dad and I both have just been patiently waiting until you finally admitted it," she continued. I thought over the years, remembering all the moments I had with Alayah up to this point. Despite our individual past relationships, I couldn't really deny that there were feelings for her there lingering in the back of my mind.

"Is it that obvious?" I asked her. She tilted her head to think, then looked back at me.

"I don't know about anyone else, but to me it is," she answered. I sighed for a third time.

My mom laughed a little again. I couldn't believe she was entertained by my distress. I don't think she really understood how this was wracking my brain. Or maybe I was thinking too hard. Either way, I was still just as confused as I was when I got there.

*****

"Tired of being inside yet?" I asked Alayah outside of my parents' house. I didn't really want to go back home just yet. I need some more distraction before being enclosed in four walls again. She walked over just as I was leaving out of the front door. She stood right in front of me and looked up.

"A little," she answered, scrunching her nose.

"Let's do something else," I said to her.

"Like what?" she laughed a little.

I thought for a second, looking down at her. The summer sun reflected off her brown eyes as she looked back up at me. She pushed her glasses further up her nose, waiting for me to think of something. I didn't really have any good ideas, but I pretended to think more just to stare at her a little longer.

"Let's just walk around, I guess," I finally said, and she shrugged.

"Okay," she agreed.

As we turned to walk down the sidewalk, I caught sight of my mom in the window, smiling to herself watching us. I thought about what she said, but I couldn't say anything to Alayah. She would've thought I was crazy.

It was quiet for a while as we walked. I knew what was on my mind, but I wondered what was on hers. Our hands kept brushing past each other's. I wished she would grab my hand or something, anything to give me some type of hint of how she felt, if she felt anything at all. But then again, I guess no hint was a hint, too. I put my hands down in my pockets, and she glanced up at me.

"Why are you so quiet?" She asked me.

"Why are you?" I asked back. She laughed a little and bumped my arm. I nudged her back. I don't know why this felt so awkward. Like I was fourteen with a first crush or something. I knew Alayah, she knew me, and we had walked down these sidewalks together hundreds of times before, but I couldn't help feeling what I was feeling. I checked my phone for any notifications from Liz. Nothing.

"I'll race you to the playground," Alayah challenged me after a moment.

"What? No," I laughed, "It's too hot."

"Oh, don't be boring, Luca," she said, smiling mischievously, "I'll give you a head start."

"You're the one that needs a head start, slowpoke," I said back to her. She laughed and stopped her stride. She tightened the jacket she had tied around her waist and looked down to make sure her shoelaces were alright. Then, she looked at me again.

"Last one to the slide has to buy ice cream," she announced, and I laughed at her again.

"Lay, you're not gonna win. You're slow," I joked, even though it was true. Despite her history of playing basketball and her athleticism in dancing, speed was not her strength.

"Luca, come on," she laughed, stepping closer to me. "Race me," she said again. I sighed and chuckled a little, knowing I couldn't say no to her.

"Start running," I told her.

She laughed and took off down the sidewalk, her curls swirling around wildly in the wind. I gave her a good ten seconds before I ran after her, but it wasn't long before I caught up. Her laughter echoed through the empty streets as the playground came into view.

She looked back at me, smiling, and it felt like time slowed down for a moment. I was fascinated by her face, the way she moved, the joy on her face, the sound of her laugh—and my breath left my lungs. My suppressed feelings for her were coming back full force, and there was nothing I could do about it.

Chapter 21: Alayah

Luca slowed down as we reached the playground. He was way faster than me, he could've easily beat me. I ran through the wood chips and up the child-sized steps to get to the top of the red and blue painted slide and held up my arms in victory.

"You owe me ice cream!" I shouted.

"I let you win," he said back, out of breath.

"I know you did," I put my arms down, "Why did you do that? I wanted to win fair and square."

"You wouldn't have," he said with a short laugh, "We just talked about this." He lifted his t-shirt slightly to wipe sweat from his forehead, revealing his abs underneath. I felt a bit awkward for looking but I couldn't look away. I hoped he hadn't noticed.

"You're not as fast as you think," I said, quickly thinking of a comeback to snap myself out of it. He glanced at me, a little smirk on his mouth.

"I'm coming up there," he said back, and dashed up the stairs to me. There was no where for me to run to. I made a quick move to slide down, but Luca caught me just in time. We both tumbled down the slide headfirst, laughing uncontrollably as we landed in a heap at the bottom, sending wood chips flying into the air.

"Ow," I laughed, the chips digging into my skin, "That was not supposed to happen."

"Wasn't it?" Luca said sarcastically. He laughed a little as he sat up. He picked a few wood chips from my hair and dusted his hands off. "I thought it was fun," he said.

I glanced at him, and he looked back at me with his espresso colored eyes. The warm wind tousled his hair a little, making me notice it had gotten a little longer over the past few months. Feeling a slight rush of boldness, I reached over and ran my fingers through it. He leaned a little closer to me, and I felt a flutter of something completely new: the urge to kiss him.

But I wasn't *that* bold.

"You need a haircut," I said, trying to overturn my strange feelings. Luca laughed, looking at the ground then back up at me.

"Is it bothering you?" He joked.

"Yes, actually," I joked back, taking my hand down from his head finally, "You need to cut it today."

"Today?" He laughed again, "I thought you wanted ice cream."

"I do," I said back, "We'll go to the store, then we cut your hair since all the barber shops are closed." I stood up from the ground, picking more wood chips off my legs.

"I'm not letting *you* cut it," he said back, standing up after me.

"Why not?" I asked him as we started off away from the playground and back down the sidewalk, "I won't mess it up."

"I don't know about that," he chuckled a little, grimacing.

"I can do it! Trust me," I assured him, "I'll have you looking like a young Brad Pitt in no time." He laughed out loud as he followed me.

We made it back to his car and got in, and drove to the grocery store. It was the first time we had been to the store in weeks, after mostly just getting whatever we needed delivered to the apartment complex. So, we threw our face masks on for safety and wandered around a little, running through the aisles and making up stories about strangers like we always did. We were like kids, skipping around and being goofy, just happy to be outside of the apartments.

But then as Luca and I walked back towards the freezer sections finally, I saw Cameron in the Wine & Spirits section with another girl. They were all hugged up, giggling and picking out bottles. Even with face masks on, I knew it was him. I knew him anywhere.

The girl was gorgeous, dark-skinned like him. I guess I shouldn't have been surprised, I had been blowing him off for a while. But I never thought this would be the outcome. We hadn't even officially broken up, but there he was, accepting kisses from somebody new. Literally. I watched them pull their face masks down for a moment just to kiss, and yeah. It was definitely him.

The sight hurt me for a moment, more than I thought it would, but I took a deep breath and turned the other way. Confronting him wouldn't have made sense. I had no other choice but to let it go.

"Alayah," Luca said, seeing what I saw.

"It's okay," I said to him. I could tell he wanted to say something, but he was at a loss for words just like I was. His expression looked so sorry for me, but I wasn't sorry. If anything, this confirmed everything Luca had always said about Cameron, and confirmed everything I had been feeling lately towards him.

"Lay," Luca said again, in a more comforting tone, but it seemed like he still didn't know what to say exactly.

"It's fine," I said again, shrugging it off, "Let's go get this ice cream and go." I started off in the other direction, Luca following me.

To cope, I didn't just grab one ice cream flavor. I grabbed three, along with a bunch of different toppings and candy. Luca didn't intervene, he just helped me carry everything to the check out and paid for it himself.

The car ride back home was quiet, not even a little music in the background or anything. I stared out the window, thinking. I knew I hadn't been totally receptive of his advances lately, but him cheating was not on my bingo card for the day. I guessed it was my fault. I felt like I couldn't even be mad. I wasn't mad. But he could've just told me—but on the other hand, I guess I could've just told him... Told him what? I still loved him, I think. Didn't I?

It was the principle of the thing that was upsetting me most, because honestly, seeing him with someone else almost felt like a weight lifted off my shoulders. That he was someone else's problem now. But the history we had over the last five years lingered in my mind.

When Luca and I got back to our building, the electricity was finally back on. We went to my apartment and threw the ice cream into the freezer. I rummaged through the drawers in the kitchen until I found a pair of scissors for Luca's hair. I opened and closed them in my hand, and smirked mischievously, forgetting about the horror at the grocery store for a moment. Luca looked at me, uncertainty on his face.

"Alayah, we don't have to do this," he said, still looking concerned for me.

"Luca, I'm fine," I assured him, with a little laugh, "This is your dream come true anyway. Now I have a reason to break up with him."

"I didn't want you to get hurt in the process, Alayah," he said, not finding the humor in it like I did.

"I'm not hurt," I said, but it was a half lie. I was. Just a little, but I'd get over it. Cheating was a dealbreaker for me, regardless of how long Cameron and I had been together. Luca looked at me like he didn't believe me, but I changed the subject.

"Can I cut your hair now?" I asked him. He winced a little.

"I don't know," he said, the uncertainty coming back.

"I'm not gonna make you look bad. I promise," I said to him, laughing again, "I won't even cut a lot." He sighed.

"Okay," he agreed with a defeated sigh. I smiled excitedly.

"Yay!"

Chapter 22: Luca

    I sat on the bathroom floor, leaning back against the tub as Alayah washed my hair. The retractable shower head hummed with the steady water flow, and of course she put on music for background noise. Even though she was acting normal, I felt like she was just pretending to be okay. I knew she had been slowly losing feelings for Cameron anyway, but no one deserves to be cheated on, especially not her. I didn't want to bring it up anymore, though. I didn't want her upset with me next. Although, I couldn't lie that with Cameron out of the way, it might be a little easier to tell if she was having the same thoughts as I was.

    I was surprisingly relaxed as she kneeled next to me, gently scratching through my head and singing along to the lyrics of the songs playing. I looked up at her as she leaned over me to grab the shower head. Her face so close to mine, I thought I wanted to kiss her. I wanted to kiss her at the playground, too. I wish I would've.

Rinsing all the shampoo out of my hair, she caught my gaze and smiled a little. Then, she flicked water at me and giggled. I did it back to her, the drops of water landing on her face and nose. She laughed again and turned the water off. She grabbed a towel and threw it over my whole head, her laughter continuing as she dried my hair with a playful roughness.

"You're like a golden retriever!" She joked, taking the towel away again, and I laughed out loud.

She searched through the cabinet under the sink and grabbed a blow dryer. She plugged it into the wall and turned it on. The loud noise and hot air filled the bathroom. The excitement on her face was hilarious. I would've done anything to keep her smiling, even let her cut my hair in this small bathroom on a random Thursday.

There wasn't enough room to bring a chair in, but I was too tall for her to cut while I stood up. So, she sat on top of the sink and reached up, snipping little by little.

"Come down," she said, still not quite able to reach some spots.

"How?" I laughed. She placed a hand on my shoulder and lightly pushed me down so I'd bend a little.

"Down, boy," she said, still playing off the golden retriever joke from earlier. But when she realized how it sounded, she covered her mouth and giggled hysterically.

"Alayah," I laughed, too, "You're so goofy." Weak with laughter, she leaned forward and rested her forehead on my shoulder.

"Just come down here!" She laughed, lifting her head up. I crouched down a little lower, and we were eye to eye.

She focused on my hair and I focused on her face, still wishing I could kiss her. Just one time, to see if I was as crazy as I felt. I watched her full lips move, forming words I couldn't pay attention to, and they mocked me. They looked so soft and inviting, trying not to lean in felt like an Olympic sport. I hoped she couldn't hear the way my heart was pounding. I almost let my intrusive thoughts get the best of me, but her voice knocked me out of my daze.

"Okay, you can relax now," she said. I stood up straight again, not taking my eyes from her. She smiled, proud of herself.

"Andrew Garfield is shaking in his boots. Leonardo DiCaprio is scared of you," she teased, holding the scissors up in her hand triumphantly. I laughed at her again. Looking in the mirror, she really didn't too bad. Trimmed it just enough that I looked like my regular self again.

"Sorry I doubted you," I said to her.

"You should know never to do that," she said jokingly, as she brushed stray hair strands from my shoulders. Her touch was making me nervous, and I hoped it wasn't obvious. She hopped down from the sink, headed out to the kitchen, and shouted,

"Ice cream time!"

Chapter 23: Alayah

Luca and I made a huge bowl of all the different ice creams, cookies and cream, cookie dough, and birthday cake. Drizzled caramel and chocolate syrup on top and seasoned it with sprinkles, gummy bears, cherries, and vanilla chips. It was the most grossly delicious sundae I ever ate, way too sweet and too many flavors mixing together but it was fun.

"We barely made a dent in this and I don't think I can eat anymore," I laughed as we faced each other on the couch with the bowl in the middle of us.

"Yeah, my teeth are hurting," Luca agreed, but still taking another spoonful.

"We shouldn't have piled it up so high," I said, looking at the mound of dessert in front of us.

"It was your idea," he reminded me, pointing his spoon at me.

"Didn't I tell you before to stop listening to me all the time?" I teased him, raising my eyebrows.

"Yeah, but I can't say no to you," he replied, scooping another spoonful.

"What are you talking about?" I asked him, amused by the response.

"I literally can't say no to you," he said back, chuckling a little,"Anything you wanna do, anything you ask, whatever you want. I can't tell you no, I don't know why. You haven't noticed?"

I thought back on all the many times Luca has gone along with my antics and crazy ideas throughout the years, no hesitation. Like the time we threw water balloons off the roof, hitting random people on prom night junior year. Or going ice skating a couple winters ago, even though neither of us can skate to save our lives. Or even the time I convinced him to volunteer with me at the zoo for a summer job senior year of high school. I thought it was funny.

"You shouldn't have told me that because now I'm not gonna let you do it anymore," I said to him, laughing a little, "You can absolutely say no to things."

"No, it's not that I don't wanna do anything you suggest. I just like seeing you happy. So, literally whatever you want, I'm all for it. No regrets," he said, a hint of a smirk crossing his face. I just stared at him for a moment, unable to tell if he was joking or not.

"Are you for real?" I asked him, and he glanced up from the ice cream bowl to look at me.

"As a heart attack," he replied, "You're my best friend, why wouldn't I support all your shenanigans?"

"You make a good point there," I laughed a little, then paused. "That was really sweet, Luca. But you're always sweet," I said after a second, admiring him for a moment. Whatever it was that was attracting me to him now, it was stronger in that moment. He smiled to himself, then shook his head.

"Not as sweet as this ice cream. I can feel the cavities forming," he joked, and I laughed out loud.

"We'll be collecting our teeth off the floor by morning," I said back.

We stabbed our spoons into the bowl, and I took it back to the kitchen and placed it in the freezer. I shuffled back over to the couch, tensing up because now I was cold from eating the dessert. I grabbed my throw blanket and wrapped myself in it, shivering a little. Almost like it was instinctive, Luca put an arm around me, and I tried not to smile.

I took another look at his hair. Not to brag, but I did pretty good for not cutting anyone else's hair before besides my own. Honestly, the whole experience was just ploy to be close to him. Him standing in front of me at the sink like that did absolutely nothing but make me want to be near him even more.

"Admiring your work?" He joked, glancing over at me, and I giggled a little.

"Something like that," I said back. He smiled, shaking his head and then laughed again.

I grabbed the tv remote and turned it on, shuffling through the streaming apps until I got to a specific one. I put on *Catfish* again, starting from the last episode we watched the other day. Engrossed in the show, it seemed like all things Cameron left my mind for a while. But that was short lived when night fell and Luca went back over to his apartment.

Alone in my thoughts, I tossed and turned for a long time. I couldn't sleep. Seeing Cameron with someone else like that made me angry, and all of our old memories came flooding back to me. It was then I realized that I had been loving and hanging onto the wrong version of him all this time. The old him. The one that wasn't there anymore. And the old him would've never done this. I pulled out my phone to text him one last message.

"I saw you at the store kissing another girl. I'm done," it said. I sent it, then blocked his number and continued to block him on all social media apps, too. I cried into my pillow, not mourning the relationship, but feeling the pain of the betrayal.

After a while, I got up and walked out, down the hallway to Luca's apartment. I didn't know if he was up or not. It was 11:45pm and we both had work the next day. I messaged him my usual "knock, knock" and waited.

Chapter 24: Luca

When I opened the door, Alayah stood there in her oversized t-shirt, shorts and fuzzy socks, looking up at me with sad, watery eyes.

"I'm sorry. Can I come in?" She said and signed simultaneously. I grabbed her hand and pulled her inside.

I wrapped my arms around her in a tight hug, and she cried into my chest. Her body shuddered as she sobbed. I knew she had been pretending all day. I hadn't went to sleep yet, because I had a feeling she wasn't okay. After a few minutes, she lifted her head and looked up at me, more tears rolling down her face. Unfortunately, it wasn't the first time Cameron had made her cry.

I sat in her car with her outside of her house. She was too sad to go inside and she didn't want her mom to see her crying. Her eyes were red and puffy, and she barely looked at me. A few days prior, she and Cameron had a bad argument that led to him breaking up with her (the first time). That day she saw him posted up with another girl. She was trying to get herself together before going inside when she called me over to tell me what happened. There were dark clouds outside that day, and water poured from the sky.

"Blame it on the rain," I said to her lightheartedly, trying to make her laugh, but it didn't work.

"Rain doesn't make your eyes red," she said back, rolling her eyes. Then after a moment, she continued, "I just don't understand."

"Alayah," I turned to her, "He's an idiot. If you try to understand idiots, you'll catch their stupidity." I got her to giggle with that one. She wiped her eyes and sighed.

"Do you think he thinks she's better than me?" She asked.

"Who cares. If he does, that would, once again, make him an idiot," I said back.

"But I still love him," she said, new tears falling from her eyes, "Do you think I'm stupid, too?" I chuckled a little bit.

"No, you're not stupid, Lay," I said. She finally looked over at me, and the hurt in her face hurt me, too.

"Forget about him, okay?" I told her, "We'll go inside and I'll tell your mom you fell and that's why you're crying."

"She's not gonna believe that," she laughed through her sadness.

"Okay, well, I'll push you in a puddle to make it believable," I joked, and she laughed out loud.

"This is why you're my best friend," she said, wiping her eyes again, "Why are you making me laugh when I'm supposed to be crying?"

"Cause I don't wanna see you cry, especially not over a guy. That's what I'm here for," I said, opening the car door, *"Now, come on. Let's find a big enough puddle."* She laughed again.

"I'm not letting you push me in a puddle, Luca!" She exclaimed, getting out of the car with me.

"No, it's okay. I won't push you hard," I teased, walking to her.

"No, Luca! Get away from me," she laughed, running away from me.

I chased her down the sidewalk as she hysterically laughed the whole time, dodging me. The rain pelted down faster, but neither of us cared. I was just glad she was laughing. We ran all the way down to my house and back, bound to catch a cold after getting completely soaked in the rain. Such a childish moment, even though it was only about four years ago. I wished I could make her laugh like that again right now.

"I should've listened to you a long time ago," she said to me, "Thanks for not saying I told you so."

"Alayah, I would never say that to you," I said back, "It's not your fault."

"Yeah, it is," she said, walking away from me, "I'm an idiot."

"No, you're not. He is," I told her, watching her walk in circles around the living room.

"I don't even think I was in love with him anymore, but I don't know. It still hurts," she said, looking at the floor. She sighed, walking around more. "I'm sorry. I know I'm bothering you. I hope I didn't wake you up," she said after a while.

"I was already up, Lay. You don't ever bother me," I said, and she glanced up at me, "If you need me, I'm here."

"I feel like I always need you," she said back, looking back at the floor. I know she didn't mean it as a good thing, but it made me smile a little.

"Then, I'll always be here," I said back to her. She lifted her head again, meeting my eyes. I reached out my arms for her, offering another hug. She smiled softly, and walked back over to me, fitting herself perfectly into my arms.

*****

After a week or so, Alayah seemed fine, this time for real. Actually, she seemed happier, not having to worry about Cameron at all. And admittedly, it was nice not hearing her talk about how terrible he was anymore. But my feelings for her kept growing, no matter how much I tried to ignore it.

With every unanswered call and dry text from Liz, I was starting to feel the same way about her that Alayah felt about Cameron. At this point, I don't think I even expected her to respond to me. The only thing I really wanted was for her to be honest. If she didn't want to continue this relationship with me, then she should've just said that. And, with the way my attention was turning towards elsewhere, I wasn't sure if I wanted to be with her anymore either.

I sat in my room at my workspace, the faint hum of my computer running was the only sound breaking the silence. The screen in front of me mocked me with a half-finished project, but my eyes were unfocused, staring blankly back at it. My phone, face down next to the keyboard mouse, mocked me, too. I picked it up, checked it again and was met with only texts from Alayah. Nothing from Liz.

Alayah. Her smile, her laugh, and the way she had always understood me, all seemed to feel so amplified now. I remembered having feelings for her before a few times, so I knew it was possible and figured it wasn't solely just the isolation forcing me to feel the way I did, but it still felt weird. And even though I had no idea where Liz and I stood at that moment, I felt guilty for having feelings for someone else.

I thought about my memories with Liz. Our time together these few years, the way I fell for her instantly, and the way I loved her enough to think about a forever with her, all for the warmth she once had to slowly turn cold.

Confusion and frustration twisted in my mind, making it hard to focus on anything else. The uncertainty of both sides only gnawed at me when I was alone, but every time I saw Alayah's face again, everything else disappeared. How did she do that? Did she know how much she made me feel better? She couldn't have, and I wanted to tell her. But how?

Chapter 25: Alayah

A week or two passed since Cameron and I were officially done, and you know what? Thank goodness. All the other times we broke up left me confused and without closure, but this time around, I just felt free. I didn't have to deal with someone always missing calls, forgetting important details, late for dates, inattentive and unthoughtful just because we had history. And most of the history in question was garbage anyway, if I was being honest.

I hadn't seen or really talked to my few other friends in a while, other than sending a few memes and videos back and forth, but I made sure to update them about this situation. In the group chat we had, I texted in big, caps lock letters "NO LONGER A DUMMY FOR THE DREADHEAD". Immediately my friends, Nia and Keaura responded with celebration emojis and asking me what happened. I replied with a short and sweet, "he's a cheater", then they started pouring questions out.

"With who!?" Nia asked.

"How? When!?" Keaura replied after.

"I knew he was a joke," another text from Nia dinged in.

"I'm so sorry, girl," Keaura said.

After running through the rest of the story briefly, I expressed how much I wasn't upset anymore. I don't think they really believed me. They had heard this story of me being over him a thousand times, but this time I really was done.

"Soon as all this is over, we gotta hang out. I have too much tea for text and a FaceTime call," Nia texted. I agreed completely.

I wanted to tell them about Luca, and how we had gotten even closer from this, but I still wasn't quite sure what was happening. I was afraid to ask him. Even though Liz was being flaky with him, I knew he still had to love her. I was sure the way he cared about her hadn't just vanished overnight, and I didn't even know if he felt the same way I did.

There were some moments when I thought he might, like at the playground or even when we woke up on the couch together. But then I thought, no. Luca was loyalty to Liz completely, even when she seemed like she didn't want him to be, like now. I would've been very surprised if Luca even glanced at me in a way that was close to how he looked at Liz. But I couldn't lie, hanging out with him felt more intentional nowadays than it did before. Even if we were just doing nothing, sitting and being bored next to each other, it was still a good day to me.

One day he worked later than usual, and I was afraid he would tell me he was too tired to for any time together. But it was the opposite.

"My brain is fried. Help. Come over quick," his text message to me said. I smiled to myself, even giggled a little, and just about ran down the hall. Before I could knock, the door opened, and he stood there like he had been waiting for me for hours instead of just a couple minutes.

"What took you so long?" He joked, and I laughed again as I walked in.

"I literally ran!" I said back.

"Not fast enough," he joked again. I just barely tapped his shoulder with my fist, and he chuckled.

"Why'd you have to work so late?" I asked him, looking at the time on my phone that read 6pm. Usually, he was done by three or four.

"I kept getting distracted and I couldn't finish anything on time. If I didn't get done, they were gonna make me work on Saturday to finish everything and I'm not doing that," he explained, leaning against the kitchen island counter.

"You're usually fast with your stuff. What happened?" I asked him, looking at him, confused. He glanced at me, pausing for a moment, then he shook his head.

"I don't know," he finally said, "but all I wanna do is lay down." He walked over to the couch and sat down, slouching and leaning back as far as he could without actually lying down. He yawned and then looked back at me, still standing by the kitchen.

"I'm not gonna bite you. Come over here," he said jokingly. I hid my smile, and sat next to him in my usual spot on the couch. He definitely looked tired, but I was happy he still wanted me there.

"You wanna watch another scary movie—?" He asked after a while, grabbing the tv remote. He couldn't even get the full sentence out before my loud, "No!" He laughed at me, but I didn't think it was funny.

"I'm not gonna scare you," he assured me, "And I doubt the lights are going out again anytime soon." I shook my head, remembering the other night.

"No thanks," I protested, "I would like to sleep peacefully tonight if you don't mind."

"You said you slept fine," He responded with a laugh, still trying to convince me. I thought about that night again, how we shared his bed and how oddly nice it was.

"That was different. I wasn't alone," I reminded him. He paused for a moment, then glanced over at me.

"You don't have to be," he said. It caught me off guard, I wasn't expecting him to say that. Was he suggesting that I stay over again? Is that what he wanted? Regardless, he couldn't have meant it being the same way as the previous night. There was no way. As much as I wanted to say okay, I hesitated. I wasn't sure if I should.

"Does it *have* to be scary?" I asked, wincing at the thought of sitting through another terrifying film.

"No, it doesn't have to be scary, I guess," he replied, chuckling a bit, "But it would be more fun if it was." I thought for a second.

I was too afraid to ask, so I signed instead, "Can I still stay?" He smiled softly and nodded. I smiled back, thinking maybe I wasn't going insane for seeing him differently. And maybe, there *was* a chance that he felt the same, but I still couldn't tell for sure.

"I forgot my throw blanket," I said regularly, realizing I felt it behind in my eagerness to get over here.

"I have blankets," Luca said with a laugh, like I should have already known.

He stood up, walked to his room, and came back with a puffy, charcoal grey comforter in his arm. He reached for the remote again, and flipped through the streaming apps, looking for another horror film to ruin my life with. But I wasn't as uneasy as I was the first time.

After choosing a movie, he sat back down and spread the blanket out over us both. He extended his arm out behind me, making it easier for me to move a little closer to him. I could see him look over at me from the corner of my eye, but I couldn't look back. The butterflies were coming back. If I looked back at him, I knew I'd have that impulse to want to kiss him again. And I couldn't do that.

Chapter 26: Luca

Alayah and I were nestled up together again in the morning on the couch. It wasn't as strange this time, at least not for me. It felt nice having her in my arms, even as the alarm on my phone went off for work. I sat up just a little to reach to the coffee table to turn it off. Alayah shifted and woke up, sleepily looking up at me, disturbed by the loud noise. It was always at max volume so that I could still kind of hear it without my aid.

"Sorry," I said out loud to her. Talking or trying to hear anything without my hearing aid felt like holding your head underwater.

"What time is it?" She asked, but I could only read her lips for the most part. I turned my phone screen to her, showing 7:30am. She groaned and sat up all the way.

"I gotta log in at eight," she said, sleepily signing to me, "I don't want to." I laughed a bit, and sat up, too.

"Come back over when you're done," I signed back to her. I didn't really want her to leave either, but we could only be so fortunate to luck out of work once in a blue moon. She smiled through her sleepiness, collected her phone, and left out.

I sighed to myself. I didn't really know what this meant. It didn't clarify anything, not in the slightest. If it was supposed to, I missed the hint. I mean, her wanting to stay with me again felt like it should've meant something. But, on the other hand, I could've been reading into it too much. Something in my head was telling me it was the latter. And I felt that pang of guilt again.

I made my way into my room to my workspace to turn on my computer monitor and log into work. Since I had slacked so hard the previous day, I wanted to start a few minutes early.

My collaboration team was calling for a meeting already first thing, to reconvene on whatever I missed yesterday. I really wasn't in a great headspace for communicating with anyone at the moment, not with Alayah on my mind constantly. But regardless, the zoom call beeped in at 8:10. I tapped my hearing aid in, and I answered with my camera off.

My supervisor, Keith, in the group greeted me and the other four team members, and got right into what he wanted to say. He started by summarizing key points from the previous day, explaining to me how they finalized the timeline for the new software deployment and set the deadline for the next month. He also added in a few bugs in the current system that needed attention.

I couldn't help thinking this could've been an email. I gave a few "yups" and "mmhmm"'s while I went to the kitchen to throw a few freezer waffles in the toaster. When they popped up, I took them back to my room, eating them without any syrup as everyone continued to talk about things I could've figured out on my own.

I was good at my job, almost too good to the point where I was becoming important. Usually I'd get office chats and emails throughout the day of coworkers asking me questions and seeking guidance for different projects instead of asking Keith. I slack off one day and everyone loses their minds.

But at least I still had a lot of tasks to do that would keep me busy, and keeping busy would make the workday go faster. And that's exactly what I needed.

*****

It was promptly 3:07 when Alayah came back over, and she normally logged out of work at 3. I was surprised when she walked in, and she laughed at my confused expression.

"I was in a cutting mood after I cut your hair. Does it look bad?" She asked me, her hair now hanging right at her shoulders as opposed to down her back like before, and her dark brown spirals were straightened. I was taken aback by the change, I never would've thought she would cut her hair. It had been super long ever since I remembered, but I didn't think it looked bad at all. In fact, I thought the new style highlighted her beauty even more. I stared at her, and hoped she didn't take it the wrong way.

"No, I like it," I finally said, "I miss your curls, though." She smiled, her teeth showing behind her full lips.

"Don't worry. They'll be back," she assured me.

"When did you even have the time?" I asked her, knowing she worked a full day like I did.

"On my lunch break," she replied proudly.

"You and your shenanigans," I shook my head, taking a dig at the conversation we had the other day. She laughed, nudging me, then continued over to the couch.

"What are we doing today?" She asked me.

"Whatever you want," I told her. I had half a mind to tell her she could stay over again, but I chose not to. The guilt I still felt lingered, but I couldn't help that being close to Alayah made me feel good.

As she thought for a moment, my mind wandered, admiring her face and the way she talked. I shouldn't have been feeling like this.

"Luca?" Her voice snapped me out of my head.

"What?" I said, realizing I missed what she said.

"I said what do *you* wanna do?" She said back, then she laughed a little. "Can you hear me okay?" She asked and signed at the same time.

"I can hear you fine, Lay," I replied, laughing at myself.

"According to you, you always go along with my crazy plans. So, I wanna know what you wanna do," she said. I thought for a second.

"Play a game with me," I said to her, meeting her in the living room.

"Okay," she said with a shrug, "What game?" I continued to walk over to the tv and turned it on, along with my Xbox and loaded a game into it.

"You're gonna make me fight zombies!?" She exclaimed as I handed her a controller. I laughed at her and sat on the floor with my back resting again the couch.

"It's fun!" I told her.

"I don't know how to play!" She said back, her now short hair bobbing every time she moved.

"I'll show you how," I assured, looking back at her. She looked unsure, and I laughed again. "Come on, Lay. Play with me," I said again. Her hesitant expression mellowed out, and she smiled a little.

"Okay," she said, sliding off the couch and sitting next to me, "Show me what to do, Teacher Luca."

Chapter 27: Alayah

I sat crisscrossed on the floor next to Luca, who was excitedly explaining the basis of the game while I tried to get familiar with the controller. Watching him so thrilled to play this silly little game with me was honestly the cutest thing ever, and it made me all giggly again. Even though I was *not* a gamer in any way, shape, or form, his energy was rubbing off on me.

As the game progressed, he teased me—of course—for how bad I was. He occasionally paused the game and reached over, showing me which buttons to press for the best outcomes. I was not quite grasping, but we sure had a good laugh watching me try.

"I don't think you're teaching me right," I joked as my person in the game died once again.

"I think you're just not listening to me," he joked back, "How did you manage to die seven times already?" I laughed out loud as he restarted the game.

"Maybe the zombies just like me. They wanna be friends," I said with a shrug. Luca laughed out this time.

"Yeah, well, you're messing me up so you gotta get it together, Lay," he responded.

"Maybe I need a better teacher!" I shot back, covering his eyes with my hand. He dodged out of the way quickly but his person in the game lost another life. He glared at me, and I laughed at him.

"Alright, come here," he said, scooting over to me. He put his arm around me, inviting me closer, and placed his hands over mine on the controller. "Let me so you how I do it," he said.

I looked up at him, and our eyes met. For a few seconds, it seemed like the game didn't even exist and I forgot what we had even been doing. Was it mutual? It felt like it was. Even when he looked back towards the tv screen, his hands never moved from mine, guiding my movements on the controller with a gentle touch. Resting against him, I felt like I forgot how to breathe. I couldn't focus on the game anymore at all now.

"You think you got it now?" He asked me, but I hadn't been paying attention.

"Um, no," I said honestly. He chuckled and paused the game.

"We can do something else if you want to," he said to me, letting my hands go, but we were still sitting close and his arm still draped over my shoulder.

"No!" I said quickly, "I want to play with you. I'm just bad at it, but I don't care if I lose. I'm having fun." He smiled a little.

"Are you sure?" He asked, and I nodded.

"Yeah, turn it back on," I insisted, absently scooting even closer to him. His smile grew a little, and he took his arm back to grab his controller again. He restarted the game once again.

"I'm glad you don't care if you lose, cause you're about to," he teased.

"Whatever!" I laughed, sitting up a little to prep myself to do my best in the game. Our back and forth jokes continued as we dove back into the zombie world, but my mind kept going back to that brief moment when it felt like we might have been thinking the same thing.

*****

"You have to draw me a new picture," I said to Luca a little later in the evening. After what turned out to be hours of playing the Xbox, we finally got tired of it. We still sat on the floor, watching cartoons on the tv now and sharing a family-sized bag of chips.

"I want one with how my hair looks now," I continued, "And I'll clip it to my fridge right next to the other one."

"I guess you're right," he chuckled a little, "You're like a different person now."

"New hair, same shenanigans," I teased with a cheesy smile. He laughed again, throwing a couple more chips in his mouth. Then he stood up and walked to his room, coming back with his sketchbook and pencil box of drawing tools.

"Are you gonna stay still this time?" He asked teasingly, and I shrugged.

147

"No promises," I said back. He smiled, tucking a pencil behind his ear and flipping through a blank page in the book.

"I'm surprised you didn't fight me on this like before. You agreed so nicely," I continued to joke. He shook his head at me.

"I can't win with you. I already know that," he said. Then he glanced up, his eyes looking at me charmingly from under his long eyelashes.

I looked away, trying not to giggle. He turned my face back towards his, concentration already creeping into his expression, and our eyes locked for a second again.

"Can't draw your face if I can't see it," he said to me, still teasing. His hand dropped away from my cheek, and he continued to stare at me.

"Well, I can't hold still if you keep making me laugh and smile," I said, trying to tease back but my voice came out so timid. His eyebrows raised a little and he smiled slightly.

"I'm making you smile?" He asked.

"You always do," I responded, admittedly.

"I'm doing something right in this life, then," he said. I covered my face and giggled, not able to hold it in anymore. Was he flirting with me? Couldn't be. He laughed at me, grabbed the pencil from his ear and got started.

I tried to keep my expression neutral this time around, remembering how hard it was to hold a smile before, but I kept fidgeting. Every time he looked up at me, my heart raced a little more. I watched the way his eyebrows furrowed in focus and the way his left hand moved as all the little lines and curves came together on the paper. I don't know why I suggested this. I couldn't handle him staring at me. The first time it was nothing, but now, every time we caught each other's eyes, I felt giggly and nervous all at the same time.

When he was finally done, he flipped the book around to show me the finished product. I loved it more than the first one. He seemed more confident in it this time and it made me smile. He tore the page out of the book and handed it to me.

"I did my best to make it perfect," he said to me, and it made me smile even more.

"Okay, this deserves the fancy magnets," I said back to him, and he chuckled a bit.

"Probably my best work so far," he said proudly, "I've never drawn that good before."

"Not even when you drew Liz?" I asked him, referring to a few sketches of her I had seen in the book before, and he looked at me confused.

"Who?" He joked. I didn't mean to, but I laughed out loud. "I'm kidding," he said, standing up and walking over to the kitchen area.

"Are you?" I asked a little more seriously, "When's the last time you talked to her?" He sighed and shrugged.

"I don't even remember," he said, "I'm not really sure that I care anymore."

"Do you really mean that?" I said, walking over to him. I couldn't read his expression. He nodded, leaning against the counter.

"I was gonna try to call her one last time, but I know she won't answer and she doesn't want to see me," he replied, "I just wanna tell her I don't wanna do this anymore." My eyebrows raised in surprise. I don't think I thought I would ever hear him say that.

"What do you think I should do?" He asked me after a while. I thought for a moment and tried not to be biased despite the way I was feeling about him.

"Well, there's not much you can do. She's not giving you many options," I said, "but, I guess you should try to call her again and tell her how you feel. If she doesn't answer, text her. If she still doesn't answer, then you tried your best." He nodded again, agreeing with my words. He took a breath and pulled his phone from his pocket.

"Wish me luck," he said, still trying to sound lighthearted. I gave him a friendly pat on the shoulder, left down the hallway to give him a moment.

Chapter 28: Luca

I tried to call Liz twice, but of course, there was no answer and I got mad. And I didn't get mad easily. I sent a text, telling her we needed to talk right then. I wasn't going to take no for answer, but she replied surprisingly quick. She must have sensed the seriousness behind the message.

"What's wrong?" She texted back.

"Not over text. Call me back," I replied to her.

"I can't," she sent back. I exhaled sharply, my irritation rising.

"I don't know what this is, but it's not a relationship. And I don't think I want it anymore…" I texted her again.

Only seconds after she read it, her name popped up as my phone violently vibrated. Now she calls. I answered and put it on speaker because it was easier for me to hear that way.

"Why are you doing this?" She asked when I picked up. I wished she could've seen how confused I was. Me doing this?

"Liz, we haven't talked in weeks! What are even doing?" I said to her. I felt like I was yelling, and I didn't necessarily mean to but I was at my wits end. I paced around the room with my phone in my hand.

"Luke, I've just been busy. I told you. I'm sorry," she said. Hearing her voice after so long definitely tugged at my chest a little, but all the weeks of mixed signals and leaving me hanging overpowered it.

"I'm not doing this. It's not fair to me," I sighed, "You fake being sick, you gave me your ring back, you refuse to talk to me. You've been busy in the past but you've never completely ignored me before."

"I do love you, Luke. Do you still love me?" was all she said back. This was stressing me. It felt like she wasn't taking me seriously.

"I don't know," I said to her, "I tried to be patient and give you some space, but the more I try, you just leave me alone. If you don't wanna be with me anymore, I'd rather you just say that then go through all of this."

It was quiet on her end for a long time. My door creaked open, Alayah coming back in. When she noticed me on the phone, she ducked back out but I motioned for her to come back. There was nothing I couldn't say in front of her, so it didn't matter to me.

"I'm sorry, Luca," Liz said finally, her voice cracking a little, "I'm sorry I strung this along, I just wasn't sure what I wanted. I know I still love you, but I don't... I didn't want to hurt your feelings. You didn't do anything wrong, you're sweet, and you've always treated me well. But I just think I want more than this. More excitement.

Something different. Being away from you with this lockdown has made me realize that. I just didn't know how to tell you and I don't want to lose you completely. Do you think we could still be friends at some point?"

After listening to her, I felt even more angry than I had when the conversation started. Why did she drag this out for so long when she could've just told me everything the day she gave me her ring back? And to ask me if we could still be friends? I was surprised at her audacity.

"Friends?" I repeated, more harshly than I intended to, "No, Liz. We can't be friends."

"Well, then I guess this is it. I'm sorry, Luca," she replied, and before I could say anything else, she hung up.

Chapter 29: Alayah

Luca was upset, but not in a mad way. In a disappointed way. Liz's words were harsh, even as she tried to say them nicely. I could tell it hurt him. Weeks and weeks of leaving him in the dark just for this to be the outcome. I couldn't believe her. Why would she do that to him? He had been nothing but good to her from the beginning. Regardless of how she felt, he deserved her honesty a long time ago.

Usually I was good at offering comfort when he needed it, but this time, I didn't know what to say to him. I stood awkwardly by the door still, watching him. He lightly tossed his phone, and it tumbled across the floor. He paced around and sighed. Then for just a moment, it was almost like a wave of relief fanned over his face. He looked at me, and me looking back at him with concern.

"Are you okay?" I asked, breaking the silence. He nodded, his demeanor relaxing a little. I walked over to him now that he seemed more approachable.

"If I makes you feel any better," I started, "*I think you're exciting.*" A smile slowly curved in the corner of his mouth.

"No, I'm not, but thanks for trying," he said back.

"Yes, you are!" I argued.

"Apparently not," he said, laughing humorlessly and walking away from me into his room.

"Ugh, Luca, don't listen to her," I said, following him, "She's missing out. Because I think you're great." Without taking a second thought, I hugged him, squeezing him in a tight bear hug. He laughed a little at the forcefulness of my embrace. He wrapped his arms around me, too, and rested his chin on top of my head.

"I think you're pretty great, too," he said back. I looked up at him, a faint smile still lingering on his face.

Would it be bad or selfish if I said I was glad he didn't have to worry about Liz anymore? Because I was. I felt guilty for thinking it, especially remembering how happy he used to be with her.

During a trip to Target, he saw her there working and even I could tell it was like love at first sight. But Luca, being the quiet guy he was, he wouldn't say anything to her. All week I went with him back to the store. Every day he was determined to talk to her, and every day he didn't do anything. I stayed at a distance, watching to see if he would finally make his move, but he chickened out every time. I remembered sitting in the car with him in the parking lot one day as he mentally prepared to go in again.

"She's gonna think you're a stalker if you don't hurry and ask her out," I teased him.

"Lay, please. You're making me lose my focus," he said back after a deep breath. I laughed at him.

"Luca, just do it! The worst she can say is no," I told him. He glanced at me.

"No, no. The worst she can say is: ew, gross, get out my face," he replied. I put my face in my hands for a second. Then he added, "I don't even know what to say."

"Tell her she's pretty and ask for her number," I told him, "She has really pretty blue eyes, tell her that. She definitely looked at you yesterday when we were here."

"Really?" He asked, his confidence rising a little. I nodded exaggeratedly.

"Yes, Luca. I don't think she's gonna say no," I said. He took another deep breath and opened the car door.

"Okay, let's go," he said. I got out with him, and we walked into the store. We roamed around for a while, searching for Liz, if she was even there. When he finally saw her, fixing a game display in the electronics section, he turned right back around.

"Never mind, I can't do this," he said.

"Oh, my gosh. Hold please," I laughed, fed up with his back and forth. I started walking towards Liz myself.

"Alayah, don't!" He called after me.

"Too late," I said in a singsong voice, looking back at him. I marched right up to Liz and smiled friendly.

"Hey, girl, hey," I said to her. She looked at me, matching my polite smile. She was a little taller than me, and slender with bright blue eyes and dark hair tied in a high ponytail. I glanced at her name tag so I could tell Luca later.

"Hey, can I help you?" She said back.

"Actually, yes," I said, "You see my friend, Luca, over there? The one pretending to be interested in the shoes on that rack?" Liz laughed, seeing me point to Luca, who's poor acting skills made him stick out like a sore thumb.

"Yeah, I've seen you guys in before," she said.

"Well, he really likes you," I told her, "He's dragged me in here with him about eight times in the last two weeks so he could talk to you, but he's a little shy." Liz giggled in her hand.

"That's so funny. He's so cute, but I thought you guys were together or something since you're always here together," she said back.

"Oh, no, we're just really good friends. Since like before preschool," I explained to her, then continued, "He thinks you're really pretty." She laughed again.

"Well, in that case," she started, "give him my number for me?"

"Of course," I smiled. She took a pen from behind her ear and a ripped off piece of paper from her pocket and wrote her number done and handed it to me. I skipped over to Luca and gave him the paper.

"Don't say I've never done anything for you, friend," I said to him. His smiled was unmistakable, but he shook his head at me.

"You're crazy," he said to me.

"You're welcome," I sang again, then we started off through the store and back to the parking lot.

Seeing him disappointed like this at her words made me mad that she would even hurt him like that. Luca, of all people, didn't deserve that. But, like I said, there was a big part of me that was glad he wouldn't constantly worry about her anymore and whether she would answer him or not. I wanted to be the one he thought about, not her.

Chapter 30: Luca

With Liz was out of my life, the guilt of spending so much time with Alayah had vanished. The way was cleared for me to explore my feelings for her without restraint. The only thing that lingered was the question of whether she felt the same. I was still too afraid to ask her. I didn't want to ruin what we had already and make things awkward. I was enjoying this time with her. I didn't want to mess it up. She was more outgoing than I was anyway. So, if she did feel the same way, I was counting on her to say something before I did.

By September, a good bit of all the lockdown restrictions were lifting, but Alayah and I still preferred the safety and comfort of each other's company. With her, it didn't feel like a lockdown anymore anyway. It never had even from the start of it, but definitely now.

For the first time in a while, she and I sat outside in the common area of the complex. The owners of the building had closed it off, but now that things were slowly trying to get normal again, they finally opened it. We weren't the only ones with the idea in mind, though. There were a few other people out there, too, but at a decent enough distance to keep any unwanted contact away.

Alayah sat across from me at a picnic table in the grass, her attention focused on a crossword puzzle she had been working on. Pen in her hand and concentration on her face, she looked adorable. Her now short hair looked like a pompom in its ponytail, all the stray curls that were too short for the hair tie floated around her ears and down the back of her neck.

"Oh, duh!" She gasped as she figured out another answer. I was amused by her dedication to an old magazine puzzle. She looked up at me. "Why are you laughing?" She asked, signing at the same time.

I couldn't remember the last time I used my hearing aid. Sometimes it was just more comfortable without it. And while I still had a tiny piece of my hearing left, I wanted to appreciate it before it gradually diminished for good.

"You're funny. That's all," I replied, signing back.

"This is entertaining. I told you that you should've done this with me," she said back. Her signing perfectly fluid even with the pen in her hand. I chuckled a little. She shivered a bit at the breeze. It wasn't quite Fall yet, but the weather had already started to change.

"Come sit over here," I told her.

Without hesitation, she got up and walked around the table to sit next to me. She slid close instinctively and tucked her free hand into her sweatshirt sleeve, continuing to work on her crossword. The warmth of her next to me made a wave of contentment come over me. Having her close was starting to be my new favorite feeling.

I watched her still and wondered if she liked being near me as much as I did. She glanced up at me, catching me staring, and giggled a little.

"What are you looking at?" She said and signed.

"Nothing," I said back, laughing at myself for getting caught even though it wasn't the first time.

We sat out there for a while, an hour or two, before we went back inside. Alayah stood close by me even in the elevator, absently moving her shoulders to the generic music from overhead. The elevator stopped on our floor and the doors glided open. The carpeted floor muffled our footsteps as we walked down the hallway to her apartment. She unlocked the door and I followed her in.

She kicked her shoes off by the door and I did the same. She sighed in relief as if she was glad to be back inside, and it made me laugh. She turned to me and made a face.

"You're laughing at me a lot today," she said with her voice and hands.

"I told you. You're funny," I said again, signing back, too. She rolled her eyes playfully and shuffled over to the kitchen in her different color socks. Just before she could open the fridge, she threw her head back and groaned.

"Ugh, I forgot I need to wash clothes," she said, "I wanted to do it before we went outside and I forgot." She looked at me, and smiled hopefully, "Can you come with me?"

"Sure, Lay," I laughed once again. She hated going down to the laundry room by herself. She said it was creepy. I guess I couldn't blame her. It was all the way down at the furthest end of the hall, with dim lighting and hospital-green painted tile walls.

She went into her room and came back with a hamper half filled with clothes and a fistful of quarters. I carried her hamper for her and we headed back down the hall. When we got there, Alayah's mood automatically tensed. Her eyes darted around the room and she tiptoed in carefully. The mixed-matched, clunky machines lined the walls and there was a wet floor sign in the corner. The pale green tiles were chipped in places, and the fluorescent lights flickered occasionally, adding to the unsettling atmosphere.

"I feel like I'm in the *Saw* movies," she signed, her voice echoing slightly in the empty room.

"Lay, there's nothing in here but a bad paint job. And they really should replace these lights," I assured her, but she was not convinced. Her eyes continued to scan the room as she loaded her clothes in, like she was expecting something to jump out at her.

"Well, this room makes me feel gross. Like the swamp monster is on his way," she responded, and I laughed at her.

"I won't let anything happen to you, Lay," I said to her.

"Oh, wow. My hero," she joked with slight sarcasm in her voice.

"Or I can leave you here," I replied, backing out the room.

"No! No, no," she laughed, ready to run after me, "Don't leave me."

"I'm kidding. I'm not gonna leave you. I like being stuck with you too much," I said jokingly, but I was actually serious. I don't even think I meant to say it out loud, but it wouldn't have been the first time I couldn't contain my thoughts about her. It made her smile, though, and she looked up at me.

"I like being stuck with you, too," she said back, nudging me a little, "If you can even call it that. You don't *have* to hang out with me every day."

"I know," I said, getting a little closer to her, "but, I want to." Her smile grew, even though she tried to hide it. The washer started, filling the room with its loud sloshing noises. We lingered there for a moment as I tried to read her grin a little more.

"Can we get out of here?" She asked after a while, "It's still creepy." I chuckled and shook my head at her. She quickly walked past me and back out into the hall. I followed her, trailing a bit behind. I wanted her to know how I felt about her so bad, but part of me just couldn't tell her.

Chapter 31: Alayah

While we waited for my clothes to wash, we stopped past his apartment so he could get his aid, even though he hadn't used it in a couple weeks seemed like. We went back to my place, and talked in my room. The sun shining through my dark pink curtains casted a colorful tint around the walls. I lounged on my stomach, my feet casually swinging in the air occasionally brushing against the headboard. Luca was sprawled out on his back, his body slightly diagonal from mine with one foot dangling off the edge of the bed. He used my throw blanket as a pillow, and kept tossing my actual pillow in the air and catching it.

Our faces were close as we talked, conversations flowing effortlessly per usual. I thought by now we would have run out of things to talk about, but I was wrong. I looked at him, watching him laugh and noticing the way his thick eyebrows slightly raised whenever he glanced at me.

Whether we were talking or signing or both or nothing at all, I appreciated these moments and the slight shift in our friendship now that we were both no longer in crappy relationships anymore. It had been years since he and I were single at the same time. He seemed happier without worrying about Liz. And I guess I was happy I had him to myself.

"What's on your mind, Lay?" He asked me with a laugh. I hadn't even noticed I was smiling looking at him.

"Remember when you had braces?" I said back, secretly admiring his prince-charming smile once again. He laughed again.

"How could I forget? Worst two years of my life. Who gets braces in college?" He said.

"I thought you looked cute," I told him, a confession I had never told him before.

"You must think I'm hot now then," he joked, throwing the pillow in the air and catching it again. I giggled, covering my blushing face with my hands.

"Well, I mean you still are cute," I admitted, literally gritting my teeth trying not to giggle again. He smiled a little and glanced at me.

"I think you're cute," he said back, "That wasn't a secret, though. You've been beautiful our whole lives." I could've screamed.

"You never told me that," I said to him, my grin way too big for my face.

"Told you what? That I think you're pretty?" He asked, "Well, I do. I always have."

"Is that why you stare at me all the time?" I teased him, and he looked at me like I had I just caught him red handed in a crime. Then, he laughed nervously.

"Maybe," he said, throwing the pillow in the air again, and catching it. My smile grew even more.

"Do you remember when you fell in the pool? At that birthday party in fifth grade?" He asked me after a while, changing the subject.

"Oh, you just had to bring that up," I scoffed, "That was not funny."

"It *was* funny. I don't know why that just popped in my head, but it was hilarious," he said back, laughing.

"I could've died!" I said, sitting up straight.

"Alayah, you were in the three-foot part of the pool. You were not in any danger. All you had to do was stand up," he laughed, and sat up, too, to see me better.

"Well, you jumped in to save me anyway," I reminded him, and smiled a little remembering the day.

"You were causing a scene," he teased, tossing the pillow at me, "You were screaming and splashing and the lifeguard was taking too long. She was probably waiting for you to just stand up, too. I had to get a new hearing aid because of you."

"Why would you wear it to the pool, Luca?" I teased back.

"Was I just supposed to suffer?" He laughed.

"Yes!" I joked, throwing the pillow back at him. He laid back down again, still chuckling to himself. I thought for a second, scanning my brain for another funny memory.

"I remember strength-training gym class in tenth grade," I started, sitting crisscrossed, "And we used to goof off the whole time because Mr. Yadery would just leave the entire class alone for long periods of time."

"They should've fired him, he was the worst," Luca cracked up, thinking about it, "He did everything except watch us like he was supposed to."

"We would just sit in under the bleachers and talk, or wander down the hallway. He didn't even know we were gone," I said, laughing.

"And he still passed us with flying colors. A-plus for gym class every time," Luca said, and I laughed some more.

"I remember when you almost ripped your arms off trying to lift the fifty-pound dumbbells," I teased, laying back on my stomach a little closer to him.

"That was not my finest moment," Luca shook his head, "I was very frail and lanky back then. I could do it now, though."

"Could you? I don't know about that," I continued to joke, almost flirting a little.

"Fifty pounds isn't a lot at all," he chuckled, "I could lift you, easily."

"Okay," I said teasingly, "Prove it, Mr. Hulk-Strength." He glanced at me with a mischievous smirk, accepting the challenge. We both stood up and he walked over to me.

"I'm not gonna jump to help you either because that's cheating," I said to him.

"I don't need you to jump, Alayah," he laughed.

"Are you sure? Cause I'm pretty certain this isolation put, like, ten pounds on me," I told him.

"I can't tell," he said back, looking me up and down briefly. Oof.

"Don't drop me," I teased.

"I'm not gonna drop you," he chuckled again.

I placed my hands on his shoulders, prepping for whatever happened next. Without any type of strain or real effort, he picked me up off the floor. I giggled, instinctively wrapping my arms around his neck as he pulled me closer.

His hands moved from my waist to just under my thighs, holding me up as my legs dangled by his sides. The nonsensical moment shifted and felt a little more flirtatious than anything. Being held by him like this made my heart race.

"Hey, I can look at you without breaking my neck," I joked, "The weather is so nice up here." Luca laughed at me.

"And you thought I was gonna drop you," he said, raising an eyebrow at me. I giggled again, our eyes meeting. And for a second, the thought of our lips touching crossed my mind again. *If I could just lean in, just a little more,* I thought, *No, how awkward would that be? I can't do that.*

"I gotta switch my clothes to the dryer," I said after a second. Luca still stared at me for a moment before saying anything.

"Okay," he responded. Then, continued to carry me out of the room and down the hall. I laughed, holding onto him a little tighter until we reached the laundry room. He placed me back on my feet gently, and I switched my clothes from the washer to the dryer, too giddy to even remember that I was afraid of going in there.

"Can you carry me back?" I asked him after starting the dryer. He smiled a little, and stepped closer to me. I put my arms around his neck again and he lifted me, carrying me all the way back to my apartment.

Chapter 32: Luca

    Alayah and I rarely ever asked to come over to each other anymore, more like just showing up and giving each other the spare keys to both of our apartments. It was easier that way anyway, especially considering all the times she had been knocking and I couldn't hear her or wasn't near my phone to know she was there. She took pride in having my other key, even painted it pink with nail polish and kept it tucked in her clear iPhone case so she wouldn't lose it.

    She was with me all the time now, and I didn't mind. Other than the hours we worked, you could count on the fact that we were together. But even while we were on the clock, we would text back and forth and eat lunch together on our breaks.

    We ate meals together more often whether we made them or ordered something. We played board games and card games and made up games, talking for hours or just sitting in a comfortable silence with each other there. If we got bored enough, we would walk through the halls of the building or take a car ride for a change of scenery. The constant company made isolation from the rest of the world seem less daunting and we definitely got closer than we ever had been.

"Luca!" Alayah's voice called as she came through my door. I laughed as I logged out of work on my computer.

Somehow I had developed a new admiration for the way she said my name. She had a distinct, singsong way of calling me. It almost started to be like a comfort thing for me, too. Like the way people have a comfort show or a favorite shirt. Alayah saying my name became like a favorite sound, even with my broken ears.

"Luca!" She said again, meeting me in my room, "Oh, sorry. I didn't know you were still working."

"No, I'm done," I told her, leaning back in my office-style wheelie chair. "Why are you screaming?" I teased.

"I didn't know if you had your aids in or not. I wanted to make sure you could hear me," she said from the doorway. When I got a good look at her, I was confused.

"Where are you going?" I asked her, seeing her dressed in jeans, a sweater and sneakers. Half her hair was pulled up neatly, the rest hanging at her shoulders. I hadn't seen her wear anything other than lounge clothes in weeks.

"That's what I was coming to tell you," she said, her eyes wide with excitement, "Guess what's open again!"

"What?" I laughed again.

"The bar and grill restaurant downtown!" She said, "Nia told me she went with her mom the other day and they're letting people eat inside now. And when you get to your table you don't have to wear a mask anymore."

"And you wanna go?" I asked her, amused by her cheerfulness.

"I just thought it'd be cool to get out of here for a little," she said back, "but, if you don't want to, if you're uncomfortable being around people, we don't have to."

"But you got dressed anyway hoping I'd say yes?" I teased her again.

"I'm not gonna force you if you don't want to, Luca," she replied in a more serious tone. I smiled a little and stood up from my chair.

"I'm messing with you, Lay," I told her, "I'll get dressed." Her grin came back and she turned into the living room to wait for me.

****

Alayah skipped through the parking lot into the restaurant, and even with a mask on her face, I could still see how hard she was smiling. I followed behind her, up to the hostess podium where there was a "Please Seat Yourself And We'll Be Right With You" sign. Alayah kept bopping through the restaurant until she found a taller table with bar stool chairs, and sat down. I sat across from her and took my mask off my face.

"I feel so normal," she said, taking hers off, too. I laughed at her. There weren't too many other people there, and the ones that were there were scattered far away from us.

A few minutes later, the waiter walked over to us and introduced himself before handing us menus. After jotting down our drink orders, he walked away, leaving us to look over the menus. It seemed like Alayah couldn't sit still. She danced a little in her seat, her fingers tapping rhythmically on the table surface, her shoulders raising and falling to her own beat. I watched her, smiling.

The waiter returned with her iced tea and my orange soda, then took our food orders. It wasn't the first time Alayah and I had been there, and she always got the same thing: Philly cheesesteak and fries. She made fun of me because I always wanted the spicy mac&cheese with honey pepper chicken tenders.

"Ugh, too hot," she said, fake gagging as the waiter walked away again.

"You're not the one eating it," I said back, flicking my straw paper at her, "Leave me alone." She laughed and threw it back at me. When our food came, Alayah danced more, picking up a French fry and biting into it.

"Wow, I missed this," she said, then taking another bite.

I laughed at her again, seeing her so happy just to be at this casual restaurant was amusing. She was so cute, sitting across from me. Every time I looked at her, she seemed even more beautiful. I looked away, not wanting her to catch me staring again. But then, I laughed thinking about another time we were here as teenagers.

"Why are you laughing at me?" She asked, glancing up at me.

"Do you remember when we came here after my baseball game right after we lost to Northridge?" I asked her, "And you laughed so hard, sprite came out your nose."

Alayah's laugh was hysterical as the memory came back to her.

"That was your fault!" She giggled, "You told that dad joke about the pirate and I lost it!"

"That was one of my best ones," I chuckled, "I think I read it on a gum wrapper or something. Want me to tell it again?"

"No!" She continued to laugh, "I don't need anything coming out of my nose again."

"Oh, come on. I think it'll be funny," I joked, taking a bite of my food, "You have tea this time, it won't burn as much."

"Luca!" She laughed out loud, and I smiled at her. Before, joking around was a normal thing, but now, making her laugh was fun for me. I loved watching her laugh.

"I'm just teasing you," I told her. She looked at me with mock irritation, then she grabbed her spoon, reached over to my plate and took a bite of the mac&cheese.

"I thought you said it was too spicy," I said to her, but before I could finish my sentence, she was already reaching for her cup.

"Help," she said, after sipping it for a while, and choked out a laugh, "I wanted to try it, but that was a mistake." I chuckled, and took a few of her fries and threw them in my mouth.

"Now we're even," I said back. She laughed, drinking from her cup again.

"I guess so," she replied. I smiled at her again, and she smiled back, giggling into the palm of her hand.

I wondered if she knew that I had been slowly falling in love with her, but she couldn't have known. A part of me wished that I could read her mind, so I could know if it was safe to tell her. I found myself flirting with her more and more every day, it was getting harder to mask my feelings for her.

"Alayah?" I said to her after a while, feeling a burst of confidence for a moment. I had half a mind to just say it.

"Yeah?" She said. When her dreamy, brown eyes looked up to meet mine, that confidence quickly vanished. The words I had in my mind completely scattered. I was stuck.

"What is it, Luca?" She asked me, while I struggled to piece together my thoughts.

"Never mind," I shook my head, "Lost my train of thought." She glanced at me like she didn't believe me, but she didn't press any further. I sighed quietly, letting the moment pass. I could've kicked myself.

Chapter 33: Alayah

"You know, bringing up all those old memories earlier made me think about when they forced us to ballroom dance in music class," I said to Luca once we were back in my apartment, "Do you remember that? In eighth grade?"

"Yeah, that was weird," he said back, facing me on the couch, "And we all hated it. Well, except for you."

"You are right about that," I agreed. Then, an idea crossed my mind. Luca noticed the wheels turning in my head and the sly smile on my face, and quickly shook his head.

"No," he said. I laughed out loud.

"You don't wanna dance with me?" I asked, teasingly, "It's been a long time!"

"You know I can't dance," he said back, chuckling a little, "I don't even remember those steps they taught us. That was over ten years ago."

"Well, I remember them! I still know how to waltz. And I remember all the routines from Swan Lake in tenth grade. I haven't had a dance partner in months. You know the studio closed indefinitely because of this pandemic," I rambled on.

Before the virus swept through, I would take dance class at the studio down town to keep up with it. I had loved to dance since I was kid. All the school productions, you could count on the fact that I was in them. Even in college, I was on the dance team. It was my thing. And other than the dancing I did in my living room on occasion, I was having withdrawals.

"In what world do you think I can waltz?" Luca looked at me perplexed. I jumped up from the couch and picked a song from a playlist on my phone.

"I'll teach you," I smiled, then continued to joke, "You can't say no to me, remember?" A big smile spread across Luca's face as he laughed at me, and it made me laugh.

"I should've never told you that," he said, standing up. I laughed a little, and helped him move my furniture out of the way so we had more space. I turned the volume of the music as far up as it would go, and started my attempt at this makeshift dance class.

"Okay, ready?" I said to him.

"No," he said jokingly again. I stepped closer to him and grabbed his wrist to place it at my waist.

"Your hand goes here," I said, suddenly nervous by his touch, then I put my hand on his shoulder, "and mine goes here."

"I know that much," he said slyly, holding up his other hand for me to take. I nudged him and slid my hand into his. I glanced up at him, his eyes already on me, waiting for my instruction. This was supposed to fun, but now the butterflies were fighting in my stomach again.

"Okay, step forward with your right foot first," I said to him after a quick exhale. He paused for a second, as if he forgot which foot was which. Then, he did it, me stepping backwards to mirror him.

"Now, your left foot follows," I continued, and we stepped in sync again. The carpet made it a little hard to move around, our feet getting hung up on the plush material. As I kept my instruction going, Luca's moves were clumsy and unsure, but I thought it was adorable.

"Stop laughing at me," he teased after a while.

"I'm not laughing at you. You're so cute," I said back, even though my giggles were punctuating my words.

We stumbled around more, laughing and completely ignoring the choreography at hand as the music replayed. Making things more hilarious, I stood on his feet on purpose, my bare feet on top of his socks, having him carry us both around the room. His awkwardness disappeared a little as he pulled me closer to him, and I wrapped both my arms around his neck. It was more of a regular slow dance than anything else by now, but the pressure of perfect steps was gone and our focus was just having fun.

Our faces were so close, I felt nervous again. The jokes and the teasing subsided as the mood shifted slightly to lingering glances and softer smiles. For the first time this whole time, it seemed like whatever this feeling was, was mutual. But, I still didn't want to say anything. I liked this moment too much to potentially ruin it. Although, I wanted kiss him or I wished he would kiss me. But then, the music on my phone stopped abruptly as a spam call came through.

Luca and I separated, and I stepped down from his feet to grab my phone from the couch. I declined the call and turned the music off when it resumed.

"Rude," I mumbled, shoving my phone in my back pocket. Luca chuckled a little.

"Since you made me dance, you owe me video game time," he said to me.

"I'm not good at your video games," I responded, and he looked at me like that was the point.

"I'm not a good dancer but here we are," he laughed, and I laughed a little, too.

"Thanks for letting me drag you into it," I said back. He sighed, then smiled at me.

"Can't say no to you, Lay. You know I'll do anything for you," he said, then headed towards the door, purposely brushing past me on his way over. I smiled to myself, and turned to follow him out the door and down the hall.

Chapter 34: Luca

So, maybe I wasn't imagining things, because with the tension in that moment, I knew for a fact I wasn't the only one who felt it. I should've just kissed her like I wanted to, but regardless of her phone ringing, I probably would've chickened out anyway. But I told myself that if another opportunity presented itself, then I'd do it.

Maybe.

A few days later, we sat on the floor in my living room playing another game. We had already went through a very long round of Monopoly, and a few rounds of Operation. The amount of games we had now was pretty ridiculous, honestly, buying a new one almost every week to occupy our time. The newest one was Perfection. We had played it a thousand times as kids, but it never got old. We took turns, seeing which one of us could beat the timer faster.

I started the timer again for Alayah's turn, turning it all the way around to the full thirty seconds. She was ready when it began counting down, a look of amusement on her face as she fumbled around with the tiny yellow game pieces trying to fit them in their respective spots quickly.

"Ten seconds, Lay," I announced to her.

"Oh, my gosh, no," she giggled, picking up the pieces more frantically.

She almost had it with only three pieces to go. But then, the timer abruptly stopped, the game popped up forcefully and sent all the game pieces flying into the air. Alayah screamed, then burst out laughing at herself. As many times as we played this game, the surprise still caught her off guard every time. I shook my head at her and laughed.

"You're silly," I told her. She continued to laugh, then gathered all the pieces together.

"Okay, your turn," she said to me.

She started the timer, and sat back to watch me with a smile still her on face, giggling occasionally as she anticipated the pop. I only had one more piece before the timer stopped and everything launched into the air. Alayah screamed again, followed by more laughter. She laughed so hard she threw herself backwards on the floor.

"I technically won. I only had one piece left. You had three," I said to her.

"Oh, whatever," she said through her laughter, "Let's play again."

"So you can keep screaming?" I teased her.

"It's funny!" She said, sitting up again, her short curls bouncing around as she giggled.

"*You're* funny, Alayah," I joked, glancing at her with a smile.

"Thank you," she said back, smiling back slyly, gathering the game pieces again, "Let's play again, but this time, we do it together. See if we can beat the timer with both of us playing at the same time."

"Let's go for it," I told her. With an excited smile, she started the timer again. We both dove right into the task, laughing as our hands kept bumping and getting tangled scrambling to put the pieces where they belonged. With only a few seconds to spare, we actually made it in time, no piece left out. But, Alayah wouldn't let me stop the timer, wanting to see the pieces fly again.

"How old are you?" I joked with her, watching her scream again as the game popped up. She laughed out loud again.

"Honestly, I'm probably still like twelve," she replied, but I shook my head.

"That's a stretch. I'd say eight," I teased, picking up the pieces and tossing them in the game box.

"Well, if I'm eight then you're seven," she said back.

"That's not accurate," I chuckled.

"You think you're more mature than me? I'm older than you," she said matter-of-factly.

"Only by a month," I reminded her, continuing to put the game away and stack it away on the tv stand with the other board games.

"Doesn't matter. I was on the earth four weeks before you. So, I am four weeks wiser," she said jokingly. I laughed at her.

"Well, I'm four weeks taller, so," I teased, walking over to the kitchen. She just about cackled, following me over.

"Height has nothing to do with age," she said back.

"You're just saying that because your short," I shot back, poking at her more to make her laugh.

"I'm not short!" She laughed, looking at me like she was offended.

"Yeah, you are," I laughed, too, "If I look straight ahead, I can't even see you."

She giggled more, standing in front of me while I looked right over her head. She stood on her toes, trying to see eye to eye with me but she was still short, her 5'4 height to my 6'1. I chuckled a little, she was so cute.

"I remember when you first started getting taller than me," she said after a minute, "I was mad. And then that summer when you and your parents went to North Carolina, and you came back like five inches taller, I was like what the heck? What were they feeding you over there?"

I laughed at her, but my mind drifted back to that summer right before we started high school for a different reason. That was the same summer my voice started to change and the same summer my feelings for her took a more serious turn. Her hair was way longer back then, down to her waist but she always wore it in a high ponytail to keep it out of her face. Her body had new curves I hadn't noticed before—probably just because we had spent so much time with each other that I never looked at her like that before then—but I remembered how caught off guard I felt, realizing how beautiful she was.

Even now, as she stood in front of me, I couldn't help but admire how those curves had only become more apparent and attractive over time. For a second, I completely zoned out, imagining her wrapping her arms around my neck like she had the other day dancing in her apartment, and me leaning close to her, our noses grazing against each other's, waiting for our lips to touch…

"Luca," she said waving her hand in front of my face, snapping me out of the daydream.

"Huh?" I said, and she laughed a little bit.

"You tuned me out? Am I talking too much?" She joked.

"No, sorry. I was just…never mind," I stumbled.

"What? You were just what?" She asked, looking up at me like she was trying to see through my mind.

"I was just thinking," I said back. She stood on her toes again for a second, still trying to level with me, and it made me laugh a little.

"About what?" She asked.

"Um," I stumbled around in my thoughts again, hoping maybe I'd finally tell her this time. But I was too afraid again. "Nothing," I sighed. Her eyebrows pulled together a little, but a smile still lingered on her face.

"You can tell me anything, Luca. Did you forget?" She said to me.

"I know, but it's nothing. Nothing important," I replied, but her eyes still locked with mine, almost as if she was trying to lure the information out of me. But the eye contact made my heart race, and if I didn't do something, I was going to explode.

"Stop looking at me like that," I said, walking away from her.

"Like what?" She asked, her expression perplexed and amused at the same time.

"Like that," I said back, pacing around the room. Why couldn't I just tell her?

"Are you okay?" She asked me after a second, her smile fading, visibly confused by my behavior. I didn't mean to act so weird. My internal struggle was eating me alive and I felt overwhelmed in that moment. Overwhelmed and mad at myself that I couldn't bring myself to just say what I wanted to say.

"Yeah," I simply said.

"Luca, tell me what's on your mind. I can tell when something is bothering you," she said, walking over to me.

"The only thing bothering me is you," came out my mouth, and it was the farthest thing that I meant to say. Her eyebrows raised, and then her expression turned sad. "Alayah. I didn't mean it like that. That's not what I meant to say," I responded quickly.

"How did you mean it then?" She asked. I don't think I had ever heard her voice so quiet in my entire life. I couldn't answer her without telling the truth, and I still couldn't bring myself to form the words. She took my silence as a response, and turned to leave out. I followed her down the hallway.

"Lay, I didn't mean it like that!" I said after her.

"I thought you liked hanging out with me all the time," she said, barely turning around to talk.

"I do!" I replied, catching her hand as she reached her door, "I do."

"Then why did you say that?" She asked me, looking at the floor.

"I just have a lot on my mind. I swear, I didn't mean that," I told her.

"Then what did you mean?" She asked me again, folding her arms and looking up at me finally. Her eyes looked so sad, and I felt horrible.

"Luca," she said when I still didn't answer, "Just let me know when you're ready to talk." She quickly went inside her apartment and slammed the door. I sighed deeply and buried my face in my hands.

"I love you, Alayah," I finally said out loud in the air, "Why couldn't I say that two seconds ago?" I sighed again, and walked back down the hallway. I couldn't have been more angry at myself.

Chapter 35: Alayah

What just happened? What was that about? Luca said he didn't mean what he said, and I wanted to believe that, but what could've possibly lead to the formation of those words? He had never said anything like that to me before ever. Maybe he didn't mean it. But what was bothering him so bad that he completely switched and took it out on me?

I sat on my bed, nothing really knowing what to do with myself. I scrolled mindlessly through my phone and turned my tv on, but it wasn't a good enough distraction. His words played in my mind over and over, for three days straight. And for three days, I didn't leave my apartment, trying to entertain myself with movies and books I never finished reading. Nothing held my attention.

My phone buzzed with texts from him, but I couldn't bring myself to answer or even look at them. I just needed a minute, a second to not be mad anymore. But every time I was ready to talk to him, his words came back in to my mind and held me back. There's no way he felt the same way I did if *that's* what he had to say about me. And that fact made me sad.

At the end of the second day, I went to my mom's house, hoping she could distract me better than whatever I was doing. I needed a change of scenery anyway. The drive over somehow relaxed me, and I decided to drive around the long way for extra comfort. Finally, I pulled into my mom's driveway and walked up the porch stairs to knock on the door.

"Hey, Alayah!" She greeted me with a smile, then continued to joke, "You never surprise me anymore. What's the occasion?"

"Just tired of looking at my living room walls," I said to her as she let me in. She hugged me, and I followed her inside.

"Well, you are just in time. Wanna help me finish dinner?" She asked me, leading the way into the kitchen.

"Yeah, absolutely," I said back, a smile crossing my face.

The last time I cooked with my mom was Christmas time. She already had a pot of spaghetti noodles boiling, and it made me think of Luca and the day we made the best spaghetti ever. Ugh, maybe this was a bad idea. I watched her get the meat sauce ready and put the garlic bread in the oven. I ended up not really helping at all, just watching as she moved around the kitchen.

"What's wrong?" She asked me, seeing right through me.

"Nothing," I said, trying to perk up, but she shot me an unbelieving glance.

"Cameron didn't try to come back, did he?" She asked, and I quickly shook my head.

"Ew, no," I replied with a disgusted expression.

"What happened then?" She asked, hand on her hip.

"It's nothing, mom," I said again. I didn't want to tell her what happened. I hadn't even told her that I was starting to have feelings for Luca. And I couldn't tell her why we weren't talking without telling her that part first. She stared at me, like she was trying to take another guess at the issue. She turned her attention back to the stove.

"Is it Luca?" She asked all too easily. I sighed, and rolled my eyes. I hated her instinct. She smiled to herself, knowingly.

"Mom," I protested.

"It must have been your fault," she laughed, and I scoffed in surprise.

"Why would you assume such a thing?" I asked her, and she laughed again.

"Because Luca would never do anything to hurt you, not intentionally at least. It had to be you. What did you do to him?" She said, hand on her hips again.

"It wasn't me!" I shouted defensively, "It's what he said to me!"

"And what was that?" She asked me. I sighed again.

"Mom, I don't wanna talk about it. I came over here to not think about it. Not dissect the situation," I replied. She nodded, understandably.

"Okay, hun. I won't bug you," she said, turning off the stove burners, "Get yourself a plate and relax."

We ate together, sitting at the kitchen table. There was a content silence in the air, but I kept thinking about Luca. Not really able to enjoy the food. My mom kept her word, though. She didn't say anything else, even as I picked over my plate.

By the time I drove home, I didn't feel any better, but one thing stuck out to me. My mom saying that Luca would never hurt me intentionally. I guess I knew that. I did know that. But he *did* hurt my feelings, regardless. But I guess I would talk to him.

Chapter 36: Luca

Alayah ignoring me for so long was the worst thing that could've happened. I had never known us argue or fight or anything before, so this was a weird feeling. I hated myself for getting so mixed up and tongue tied with my thoughts and saying something I didn't mean. She had to know I didn't mean it. I missed her bad. It had only been a few of days, but after spending every day with her for months, three days seemed like forever.

I texted her, even tried to call her, but she wouldn't answer. Usually I wouldn't push or press her too much, but I couldn't handle her being mad at me. I felt like I was going crazy in the four walls of my apartment. I tried to focus on work, but I was slacking again. I attempted to distract myself with my video games, but it was a fail. I wanted to see her. I paced around the hallway, back and forth, afraid to knock on her door.

I sat out on the fire escape stairs, needing the fresh air to clear my head, but it wasn't working. I waited for her to want to talk to me again and hoped it wouldn't be too much longer so I could tell her how sorry I was, and what I really wanted to say.

I wanted to tell her how I felt about her. I wanted to tell her how much I thought about her, even when she was right in front of me. I wanted her to know how being close to her made everything so much better, how making her laugh was my favorite thing to do, how bad I just wanted to have her. But would she even believe me now?

After a while, I watched her car leaving from the parking lot. I wondered where she was going, and I upset that I couldn't ask her. I couldn't annoy her anymore with my texts and calls, though. I didn't want her to get even more mad and delay her talking to me even more.

So, I waited a little longer, hoping I didn't mess things up before they even started.

Chapter 37: Alayah

On the fourth day, I walked around my kitchen in the morning with a bowl of cereal in my hand and my throw blanket around my shoulders when there was a knock on the door. I knew it was Luca, but I didn't go over right away. I continued to eat for a second, but he knocked again.

"Alayah," he said on the other side of the door. I could hear the regret in his voice. I sighed and put my bowl in the sink. I slowly walked over to the door, but didn't open it.

"Yes?" I said back.

"I'm sorry," he said, "Can you please let me in? I miss you."

"I thought I was bothering you," I shot back. I guess I shouldn't have been petty about it, but my feelings were still hurt.

"Lay, you don't ever bother me. I didn't mean it. Please?" He replied. I sighed and opened the door finally.

He leaned against the doorway, almost like he was struggling to hold himself up, his eyes pleading. My soft spot for him immediately took over, seeing his face, and I forgot about being upset.

"I believe you," I said to him, my voice suddenly quiet.

"There's no one I'd rather spend my time with than you," he said, standing up straight, "I'm sorry, Lay." I didn't say anything else, but I slammed into him with a tight hug. I felt all the tension in his body relax as he wrapped his arms around me, too. I didn't realize how much I missed him until then.

****

Luca and I accidentally stayed up later than we planned to that night. We had spent that whole day jumping back into our usual routine, all the hard feelings melting away being back in each other's company again. We talked and joked like normal again. I missed him a lot, and I didn't want to be on bad terms with him ever again.

It was almost three in the morning when we realized how late it was, but it didn't feel like it. Luca laughed at me after I yawned, and checked the time.

"I thought we agreed not to stay up all night again," he said to me, sitting up from his lounging position on his bed.

"Time flies when you haven't seen your best friend in days," I joked back, tucking my hands into the sleeves of my sweatshirt and standing up from the bed, "It's way past my bedtime, though."

"Hey," he said, catching me before I hit the doorway. I turned back to him.

"Yeah?" I said. He hesitated slightly before speaking again.

"Just stay," he said finally after a second, "You might as well. It's late." I tried not to smile.

"Are you gonna sleep on the couch?" I asked him.

"Yeah, I will," he said, nodding. I looked at my feet and fidgeted with my sleeves more.

"What if I don't want you to?" I just barely mumbled, surprised it even came out my mouth. He chuckled a little.

"Where do you want me to sleep then?" He asked, but I was too scared to say what I wanted to say. Thankfully, though, he got the hint. He stood up and turned out the light, the glow of the streetlights outside illuminating the walls slightly. He and I both took our glasses off, and set them down on his dresser. Then, I followed him back over to his bed and we climbed in under the blanket.

"Come here," he said, reaching for me. I moved closer to him, cuddling up to him. His arm wrapped around me protectively, pulling me even closer by my waist. The warmth from the blanket and from him made me more comfortable than I wanted to admit. Sounds of distant cars outside and our own breathing filled the silence around us. The safety and contentment I felt hearing his heartbeat against my ear was so much better than anything else.

"Luca?" I said quietly, looking up at him.

"Yeah?" He looked back at me, matching my hushed tone.

"Is this weird?" I asked, our faces inches apart.

"I don't think so. Why? Do you wanna leave?" He replied.

"No. That's not why I asked," I answered back.

"Good. I don't want you to leave," he said. His response sending the butterflies in my stomach swirling out of control. He laughed quietly, his smile breaking through the darkness of the room.

"This was your idea anyway," he teased. I giggled a little, covering my face.

"I thought you didn't like sleeping with this in," I said, lightly tapping the hearing aid in his ear.

"I don't, but we can't sign in the dark," he laughed again, "Plus, I like hearing your voice without struggling. Hearing you say my name is, like, one of my favorite sounds."

"Why?" I asked.

"I don't know," he said, "I can't describe how I hear it, but I just like the way you say it." I smiled, watching him laugh. Even in the shadows, I could see he was blushing.

"That's actually really cute. I didn't know you had favorite sounds," I said back. He sighed, looking up at the ceiling.

"Yeah, I guess it's just a weird thing I keep track of mentally," he explained, "You don't know what you have until it starts fading away. Even though I have my aids, there's nothing like hearing with your own ears. And I know one day, I won't be able to at all. So I just have sounds that I'll remember even after that time comes."

Him saying that made me sad. I don't think I had ever thought of it like that. I knew he could be insecure about it every now and then, but I guess I always just figured he was used to it. I never realized how much of a mental thing it could be for him. He glanced at me again and noticed my expression.

"Don't be sad," he said to me.

"Well, I wish you didn't have to go through it," I said to him, "I've known you my whole life and I still can't imagine it."

"It's not a big deal. I don't want you to be sad for me," he said, turning to face me.

"If anybody deserves to hear and have everything that's good in life, it's you, Luca. You're the sweetest guy in the entire world," I told him. He smiled a little.

"You haven't even seen the entire world," he joked, but I was serious.

"I don't need to, to know that," I replied, reaching to run my hand through his hair and touch his face. I had never seen him look at me like he had in that moment. It felt like time stopped.

"Alayah?" He said after a moment, and I waited for him to continue, "Can I tell you something?"

"Of course, you can," I said, but there was a knot of tension in my stomach and my voice was like a whisper again.

"Even though being stuck in here wasn't ideal at first, being with you makes it so much better to the point that I don't even want to go anywhere anymore. Not without you at least," he said, "I know we've been friends for a long time, but I really care about you a lot. I love being close to you." I was surprised by his words, but a little flicker of happiness came over me knowing that we were actually on the same page this whole time.

"I feel the same way," I said back.

"Do you?" He asked, and I nodded.

"Yeah, I do. But I didn't know you felt that way, too," I told him. He got even closer to me, if that was possible.

"The other day when you asked me what was on my mind," he said, then paused for a second, "*You* were on my mind. You always are. Even when I'm with you, I'm thinking about you. So, when you said you can tell when something is bothering me, I didn't mean what I said the way it sounded. I just meant that I can't stop thinking about you, no matter how hard I try. And it's been wracking my brain for weeks."

When I finally heard his explanation, I felt so bad for ignoring him for so long. I reached over to place my hand on his face again.

"Why didn't you just tell me?" I asked him.

"I was afraid to. I didn't know how you would react if I told you I'm in love with you," he said. My eyebrows raised slightly. Those words were totally unexpected, but at the same time, it felt like I had been waiting for him to say that for so long. And I was absolutely in love with him, too.

"I love you, Alayah," he said.

"I love you, Luca," I just barely whispered back. With my heart racing, I gently pulled his face closer to mine and kissed him.

Finally.

Chapter 38

Luca:

Honestly, I didn't think I was bold enough to tell her how I felt, but I was so glad I did. Having her in my arms like this was better than I could've imagined. I was almost mad at myself for waiting so long. Her lips against mine was a feeling I had missed out on for so long, I didn't want to stop.

Alayah

The longer the kiss lingered, the more the tension grew between us. He kissed me so deeply, but his hands were hesitant. Typical Luca. So sweet, so careful.

"I want you. Can I have you?" He asked in a whisper. It ignited a spark in me.

"Of course, you can," I whispered back, my heart racing.

Luca

She moved my hands where she wanted them to go. Caressing along her legs, under her sweatshirt, my lips trailing down her neck. We shifted around, our lips still molded together. She was under me, one arm around my neck and the other taking my hand under her shirt again, up higher this time. Our breathing got heavier and she pulled me closer to her. My feelings for her were overwhelming.

Alayah

I didn't realize how much I wanted this until it was happening, and I couldn't believe it was happening. I tugged at his t-shirt, my fingers curling around the fabric with a new found sense of urgency and anticipation. He understood the gesture, and swiftly pulled his shirt over his head, tossing it to the floor. He met my eyes again, gazing at me with that look again. My heart flipped.

Luca

Alayah's hands drifted from my shoulders to my chest, tracing the contours of my body. It felt like my skin was tingling wherever her fingers were. I leaned down to her face and kissed her again, my hands wandering again but stopping to rest right at her waist. I didn't want to go any further until she told me to. She smiled a little at my caution.

"Luca," she said softly. I felt like she could read the curiosity and heavy desire I had for her. "It's okay. You can touch me," she said reassuringly, "I want you to."

Alayah

My words seemed to send a thrill through him, pushing him into a more confident nature. His arm hooked around my waist as we rolled, pulling me on top of his lap, my legs on either side of him. Our lips found each other again, and his warm, gentle hands glided over my torso, lifting my sweatshirt up, only breaking the kiss to take it over my head. His hands moved to my back, his fingertips softy caressing along my spine. It was like electricity sparking through me with every touch, like he was touching every single nerve on my body all at once.

Luca

I pulled her even closer. I kissed her from lips to her neck to her shoulder. She shrugged just slightly, a deeper exhale escaping from her parted lips. Noticing her reaction, I kissed her there again. Her shoulders raised a bit more, and she giggled quietly. I smirk crossed my face just before I kissed her lips again. She took down her bra straps and reached behind her back to unhook it, casually throwing it aside. The feeling of her bare, soft skin against mine heightened the intensity between us with every second.

Alayah

Luca's hands and lips explored the new territory of my body, softly caressing, squeezing, kissing. His touch still careful and reverent, like he was trying to memorize every curve. As sweet as his touch was, I could feel how excited he really was under me as I sat on his lap, and it turned me on even more. The heat of the moment intensified, and we shared another deep, passionate and urgent kiss that kept going. He flipped us around again, and he was on top of me. More clothes came off and hit the floor, and we tangled up together even more, Luca's touch traveling down my body with gentleness and fervor.

Luca

Alayah guided my hand again, letting me feel her between her legs. The more I touched her, the more her body responded. I watched every reaction, every breath she took, and I just wanted to make her feel good like this all the time. I kissed her from her lips to her lips, until I couldn't wait anymore. I had to have her the whole way.

Alayah

The sensation was better than any other time I had before, almost like I was hypersensitive to every movement. Forehead to forehead, perfect eye contact, I held onto him, my legs by his sides and him in between them. Every second seemed better than the last. His breathing got heavier, his touch was still gentle but somehow more assertive at the same time, his gaze more intense, his demeanor almost primal. Who was this person? I had never seen this side of him before. I mean, I liked it. A lot. It added to my arousal even more, and I couldn't hold back my voice.

Luca

"Luca," she breathed out, soft and airy. I thought I liked the way she spoke my name before, but the way she voiced it now completely changed my mind. Moans escaped her mouth even as she tried to control it. My new favorite sound. Her toes pointed and she gripped tightly onto me, scratching my back and grabbing at my hair. Her breath got faster, each inhale and exhale more sharp and pronounced than before. She looked up at me, her dreamy, brown eyes pleading for me not to stop. And I didn't, although the way her body reacted to me made it hard not to.

Alayah

After a while, I was on top again, his hands firmly placed on my hips, guiding me on him. He reached a spot I didn't even know was there. I felt like my eyes were crossing, and I was whimpering almost, rocking back and forth and up and down. I was going to burst into flames in the best way. The look in his eyes mirrored the same desire, and his low groans let me know it felt just as good for him as it did for me.

Luca

Her voice was so sweet, almost ethereal. I watched her in awe. The way her curls tousled as she dropped her head backwards, enjoying every passing moment; the way her full lips parted, every sound she made was a testament of how she was feeling; her gorgeous, brown skin glowing even in the dark. We made eye contact again, and there was a fire in her eyes I had never seen before.

"You're so beautiful," I told her, reaching up to caress her face, my thumb brushing against her lips. A smile curved in the corner of her mouth, and she tilted her head in my hand and held it there.

"I love you," she breathed back.

Chapter 39: Alayah

The brightness of the daylight woke me up. Luca's arms were wrapped tightly around me, my face cozily buried in his bare chest. The warmth of his body heat was so comforting, and I hugged him to me a little more. I lifted my head to look up at him, admiring his face; the faint freckles scattered across his nose and his lips slightly parted as he slept. His eyebrows furrowed in his deep sleep. I reached up and gently smoothed them over, and his face almost immediately relaxed as his eyes opened. A small smile crossed his mouth, sending a rush of butterflies through my stomach.

"Good morning," he said, his voice a little groggy, then a confused look took over, "Is it even morning? What time is it?"

"I don't know," I giggled a little, shrugging.

"Doesn't matter," he said, pulling me closer and closing his eyes again, "I'm not moving." I giggled again, and he kissed the top of my head before drifting back to sleep.

****

A little later after we woke up again, we hung around the kitchen (dressed again of course) deciding on breakfast even though it was probably nearing three in the afternoon. Luca leaned over the counter island, taking sips from a plastic water bottle and I casually walked around the room, thinking about what the heck just happened.

"Why are you pacing?" Luca asked, laughing at me.

"I'm not," I said back.

"You are," he said, "What's wrong?"

"Nothing's wrong, by any means," I said, way more enthusiastically than I planned, and he laughed again. "I'm just...how long have you felt—-"

"A long time," he answered before I could finish my sentence.

"How long is a long time?" I asked, leaning over the counter across from him. He thought for a second, taking another drink from his water.

"A long time," he simply repeated, smiling a bit, "My whole life."

"That's news to me!" I said, standing up straight again, "Why didn't you ever say anything?"

"I didn't think you ever saw me that way, so I just ignored it and accepted that I'd just always be your friend," he explained.

"But that doesn't make sense, you've been in plenty of other relationships, Luca," I said to him.

"Yeah I know, and I almost married somebody else because I thought I couldn't have you," he said back, and my jaw almost dropped.

"You say that like you never loved Liz," I said back to him, raising an eyebrow.

"No, I did. I'm not downplaying that," he shook his head, "I'm just saying, I had to force myself to move on because I never thought you'd see me like that. But it wasn't until months ago when we started being together more that I realized how much I really do care about you." I smiled a little, and walked over to him.

"I really wish you would've told me sooner," I said, "You didn't have to suffer." He laughed a bit. I paused for a moment, and wrapped my arms around his neck, and it reminded me of another memory.

"Do you remember junior prom?" I asked him, "And you didn't wanna slow dance with me because you afraid you'd step on my feet?" He chuckled and nodded.

"Nothing has changed," he joked. I smiled more.

"All I wanted to do was dance with my friend and you refused," I said.

"Yeah, and you got mad at me, too," he added, then continued to mock my voice, " '*Why'd you even come if you weren't gonna dance with me!*' " I laughed out loud.

"Okay but I wasn't just mad because of that," I told him, "I wanted to be close to you and you wouldn't let me." Luca looked at me confused, and I dropped my arms from around him.

"Since when?" He asked, and it made me laugh. I thought about that day:

For a afternoon in May, it wasn't very hot out. We stood in my front yard, teasing each other about how fancy

206

*we both looked. His mom and my mom were cheesing,
taking as many pictures as they possibly could and going
back and forth about their own prom. They were so excited
we were going together.*

*My red dress was long and straight, elegant and
sleeveless with sparkles from top to bottom. My mom spent
two hours flat ironing my hair that morning, and doing my
makeup perfectly. I'm pretty sure it was the first time I had
ever seen Luca in a tux, other than at his aunt's wedding
when we were kids. He was so handsome, even as he poked
jokes at me behind his hand to make me laugh for the
pictures. But I wasn't just laughing because he was being
funny, it was nervous laughing because I had this weird
feeling for him in that moment that I had never had before.*

*I remembered reaching over to straighten out his
bow tie, just for an excuse to touch him, and he gave me
this goofy grin that I thought about for the rest of the night.
It made my heart skip.*

"I mean, it was short lived," I said to Luca, coming
back from my thoughts, "But that whole day I was just like
'wow why is he cute' and I couldn't wait for the slow
songs, but then you wouldn't even do it. And I thought you
just didn't wanna be on me like that, so I forgot about it."

"You gave up too easy," he joked, and I laughed
again.

"Clearly!" I said back, and then I continued,
running a hand through his hair, "I don't know why it took
me so long to see it again."

"Well, I can't really hide my feelings for you
anymore. Obviously," he said, pulling me closer to him, "I
think it would be hard to go back to being just friends after
last night anyway."

"I don't wanna be just friends after that," I said back, my voice way too enthusiastic again.

"Good," he replied, and I giggled just as he kissed me.

"Actually where's that ring Liz didn't want? Cause I'll take it," I said jokingly, and he laughed out loud, letting me go.

"Was it that good?" He asked me.

"Yes," I simply said. Flashbacks from the night before taking over my brain, the way he touched me, the look in his eyes. There was not one place on my body his lips didn't touch. I could truthfully say no one had ever *loved* me like that in my entire adult life, taking care of every single physical need.

"Like, where did that even come from? I wouldn't have imagined all that from you," I added, still thinking about it.

"What does that mean?" He continued to laugh.

"I don't know, but that was not you. That was a different person," I told him, and a smirk slowly formed in the corner of his mouth. "Can we do it again?" I asked after a second.

"Right now?" He asked, and I nodded, "You don't wanna eat breakfast first?"

"No," I answered quickly, and it made him laugh. He leaned down and kissed me. I wrapped my arms around his neck again. He lifted me up which made me giggle, and he carried me back to his room.

Chapter 40: Luca

"Luca," Alayah's voice faintly called me, "Luca, wake up." I heard her, but couldn't bring myself to open my eyes. Her voice infiltrated my subconscious, causing me to dream about her in my half sleep state. I saw her face hovering over mine, her hair falling in front of her eyes almost in slow motion.

"Lucaaaaa," her voice sang again, then it seemed like she screamed, "Luca!" My eyes finally opened, seeing her looking up at me. I smiled at her and squeezed her tighter in my arms. She giggled into my chest and said my name again, along with some other words I couldn't make out.

"I can't hear you," I teased her, even though I really couldn't. I pulled her even closer. Her body shook with more laughter, and she popped her head up.

"Get up," she said with an amused smile on her face, her voice still a little faint to me.

"Still can't hear you," I teased again.

"Luca!" She shouted with laughter. I laughed and loosened my grip on her. "You're gonna make us both late, playing around. It's seven-twenty," she said and signed. She picked up her phone next to her and showed me the time.

"Sorry," I signed back, "You're fun to mess with." She sat up, only wearing my t-shirt, and positioned herself on my lap, a smirk curving over her lips.

"I think you just like flirting with me," she replied.

"Can't argue with that," I said back, and she giggled again. Then, she leaned down to kiss me. Any time my lips touched hers, it turned me on, and she knew it, too.

"Put your hearing ears on and clock in," she said, her eyes alluring. She kissed my cheek then got up, and grabbed her shorts from the floor to put them on.

I sat up, watching her. Even though we were officially in a relationship now, things didn't really change that much other than the intimacy and the fact that we never slept alone anymore. It seemed like we were making up for lost time the way we couldn't keep our hands off of each other.

Whether it was my apartment or hers, she never left my side until it was time for work, and even then, I didn't want her to leave. It could've been the happiness I felt finally having her to myself or the way it seemed she was so excited being with me, but I felt like a different person. I couldn't really explain it, but it was nice not hiding my feelings for her anymore. It had been a few weeks already. The switch was so natural. It wasn't awkward or anything, going from being friends for so long to being in a relationship. It just made everything better.

"See you at twelve," I told her, signing again.

"On the dot," she said and signed back, "Break time is the best time." I laughed a little as she left out, then got myself together to log in to my computer for work.

Later on, my phone rang with a call from my mom. I answered and put it on speaker so I could still type freely.

"When were you gonna tell me you and Liz really broke up this time?" She asked, cutting right to the point. I paused for a second then chuckled. Honestly, I had forgotten all about Liz.

"Sorry, it slipped my mind I guess. We broke up weeks ago," I told her, still focused on my computer screen in front of me.

"Well, I saw her yesterday at the store and looked like an idiot asking her how you guys were doing so thanks for that," she said with a laugh.

"Sorry," I said again.

"Well, thank goodness. But, how are you? I haven't heard from you in a while. You okay?" She said after a second.

"Yeah, I'm good, just working," I replied.

"Good, good. How's Alayah?" She asked. I smiled a bit at her name, and sat back in my chair.

"She's fine," I said, a little hesitant to tell her about the new development. I knew how she was going to react. "She's working right now, too. Um, she's my new girlfriend," I finally said.

"That's wonderful, Luke!" She shouted. I chuckled again, I could hear the joy in her voice. "I'm so happy for you! Glad you finally listened to me about something," she added.

"I figured you'd say that," I said back, amused by her celebration.

"Well, tell her I said hi. I won't keep you long, I know you're working. Just wanted to check on you. Talk to you later," she said.

"Talk to you later," I repeated, and then she hung up.

I looked at the time on my computer screen, 11:48. I didn't want to start anything new with only a few minutes left before my lunch break, but I also couldn't log out yet. I wasted some time, typing in random documents and excel spreadsheets until the minutes passed. And at exactly twelve, I clicked out, jumped up, and almost sprinted down the hall.

"Good timing," Alayah said with a smirk, opening her door just as I got there. Then she laughed, "Did you run?"

"Yeah, we only have an hour," I said to her, slightly out of breath.

"Only? How much time do we need?" She asked, laughing still. I smiled at her.

"More than that," I replied, grabbing her face gently and pulling her in for a kiss as I stepped inside. She giggled, pushing the door shut with her foot and walked backwards, still attached to my lips. We stumbled a little, navigating through the room with our eyes closed until the couch caught us.

Chapter 41: Alayah

A few days later, my friends Nia and Keaura were coming over. Even though we texted every day in our group chat, I hadn't seen them since before the pandemic started. Since things were slowly starting to settle, we decided we were due for some girl talk.

It was nearing four o'clock, and Luca and I had just finished a movie in my living room. As the end credits rolled, we untangled from under my throw blanket. Luca stood up and stretched, a content sigh escaping from him as he walked around the room.

"Are you sure you don't wanna just stay?" I asked him, folding my blanket neatly next to me.

Nia and Keaura had been my friends since middle school, but Luca didn't have many friends that lived close. The kids in elementary were cruel and teased him a lot because of his hearing aids, so he really didn't start making friends until high school and college. But, most of them moved out the area since. He still had one or two around, but it had been a while since he had seen them. I suggested he just stay so he wouldn't be by himself waiting for me, but he insisted he was fine.

"No, have fun with your friends, Lay," he told me, but I frowned.

"What if I miss you?" I said back, and he chuckled a little. Now that he was my boyfriend, I couldn't help but be completely infatuated with him. I hoped I wasn't being too weird or clingy, but he never seemed to mind.

"Just let me know when you want me to come back," he said.

"I don't want you to leave in the first place," I replied, standing up from the couch. He smiled and walked back over to me.

"Just don't fall asleep without me," he said, with a kiss on my forehead.

"I wouldn't dare," I said back teasingly, and he laughed again.

"I love you," he said with a little smile, walking towards the door.

"I love you, too," I told him, almost blushing. I loved when he said it to me now.

Just as he opened the door to leave out, Nia and Keaura appeared. They both said hi to him, and he greeted them back. He glanced at me one more time before turning down the hall, a sweet smile on his face, and I couldn't hide my grin.

"So, what was that?" Nia asked me, peeping the silent exchange between Luca and I.

"Yeah, that was a *look*," Keaura added, "Did we miss something?"

"Well, there has been a recent plot twist of events," I said to them as they continued through the door.

"Girl, hold on. Let me get COMFY before you say anything else," Nia said, hurrying to the couch with Keaura right behind her. I sat in my swivel chair next to the couch, laughing at their anticipation.

Nia was a little lighter than me with honey brown eyes, a round face, and hair she always kept in box braids, changing colors each time she got them done. This time they were black with blonde highlights. Keaura was a couple shades darker than me, absolutely gorgeous girl and always kept her makeup to the tens, and you'd never catch her without her hair done either.

"Okay, AJ, spill it," Keaura said, crossing her legs and folding her hands over her knee. I laughed at her calling me that nickname. She and Nia were the only ones who ever called me that, for my first and middle name, Alayah Jade.

"Well, Luca and I are dating now," I finally said. A grin spread across Keaura's face and she squealed a little, clapping.

"That's not a plot twist, that should've already happened," Nia said matter-of-factly, "But I'm so happy for you! Finally! Good gracious." Nia was one of the ones who always teased that Luca and I should've been together years ago. I used to say she was crazy. Now look.

"Wait! What happened to that girl he was literally engaged to?" Keaura asked, holding her hands up like she was stopping traffic.

"Sis was a weirdo, and she didn't deserve him if we're being honest," I admitted, "She was cool in the beginning but she got strange this year so they broke up."

"So you caught Cam cheating and ole girl was being unappreciative? Got it," Keaura said, gathering all the information in her head.

"He wasn't cheating with *her*, was he!?" Nia asked, sitting at the edge of her seat.

"Oh, no. It was somebody else, but *that* would've been a plot twist for sure," I responded, standing up to go to the kitchen, "You guys want anything? My fridge is literally loaded."

"No, I can't eat anything until I know all these details," Nia said back, "With that being said, I have to know."

"Know what?" I asked her, amused by the smirk on her face. She and Keaura gave each other a look, then looked back at me.

"How is it?" Keaura asked for her, her eyebrow raising in interest. I laughed and covered my face, but they saw right through my flustered reaction.

"It's…wow," I replied, not being able to formulate the words I wanted to use to politely explain it, "You know how people say '*Its always the quiet ones*'? Well, it's definitely the quiet ones."

With my response, Nia screamed and Keaura was laughing. I covered my face again, trying to rid myself of more flashbacks coming back to my mind.

"Not your bestie carrying a lethal weapon around this whole time!" Nia yelled in her surprise.

"That's what I was thinking!" I shouted back, and all three of us laughed. "But it's not just that," I added after a second, "He's so sweet. He's always been that way, but I don't know. He's even more sweet to me than before."

And that was true. Before now, I had never really experienced Luca's romantic side. He was a *fantastic* lover, but an even better boyfriend already—and we hadn't even left these four walls yet. He was affectionate and attentive, two things Cameron never was.

And honestly after I thought about it, I always loved Luca, too. Maybe not in the same way he did years ago, but I absolutely always cared about him and for him. He was the only friend I had that I could trust with anything, who I could tell everything to, who I could really be myself with.

I remembered how quiet and insecure he was when we were kids because of his hearing disorder, and I wanted to be there for him. Not because I felt sorry for him or anything, but because I loved him. I never wanted him to be sad, that was one of the reasons I constantly came up with crazy ideas to keep us busy and laughing. I never wanted him to feel any weight of the mean things other kids said. And now, it was just the way our friendship went, unceasingly joking and playing around. I never took him for granted, I was super appreciative to have someone like him in my life. I was excited to be with him now and see where our relationship would go.

The more I talked about him to my friends, the more I missed him already. As the subject changed and we chatted more about other things in their lives, I texted him.

"Hi, I miss you 😊," I sent to him.

"It's been thirty minutes, Lay 😂🖤," he replied.

"Okay well that doesn't make it any less true 🙄 😂," I responded back.

"I miss you too but the zombies are keeping me company until you're ready for me 🧟🎮," his next message read.

"Play with me next 🎮 😊," I flirted.

"Don't worry, I will 😵 😊," he replied, and I giggled out loud. Nia and Keaura both looked at me.

"Sorry," I laughed, tucking my phone away.

217

"You ain't gotta be sorry, sister," Nia said with a teasing smirk, "Text your man. You're not bothering me. Cause I'm sure texting mine." I laughed at her.

I was so glad we all finally met up again. I didn't realize how much I needed these laughs with them. They stayed for a while, and we ended up ordering take out, enjoying a good meal while we gossiped some more about everything we missed these past several months.

It was around ten at night when they left, and of course, I immediately changed into my comfy clothes, a t-shirt and shorts. Then, I made my way down the hall back to Luca's apartment. I unlocked the door with his spare key I had tucked in my phone case, and walked in. The living room was empty, only a single light on in the kitchen, but I noticed the faint glow of the tv coming from his dark bedroom.

I quietly shut the door, and made my way through the room, tiptoeing on the hardwood floor just in case he was sleeping. When I reached his half open bedroom door, I realized he wasn't asleep at all. He was sitting up on the bed with his back resting against the headboard, casually scrolling through his phone.

"Did you wait up for me?" I asked in a singsong voice, my face breaking into a smile.

"Maybe," he said, smiling back, "Did you have fun?"

"Yeah, but I couldn't wait to get back to you," I told him, climbing into the bed next to him. He put his phone down and embraced me as I snuggled myself close to him. He was so warm, like my personal weighted blanket. Our legs intertwined, my cold feet against his, his hand softly rubbing my thigh, and his eyes on me. I was the most comfortable I could ever be.

Chapter 42: Luca

Alayah intertwined her fingers with mine, then untangled them, then traced each one of my fingers with hers, then spread out her whole hand against mine comparing the two. She didn't know I was awake yet, but I watched her, very amused by whatever this was. Her curls fanned out over my chest, her head just under my chin.

"What are you doing?" I finally asked her. The sudden sound of my voice made her jump a little, and she looked up at me.

"How long have you been up!?" She said back, and I laughed at her, "I was just looking at how big your hands are."

"Why?" I chuckled. She sat up. Her hair fell in front of her eyes and she ran her hand through it to push it back, her other hand holding the blanket up to her bare chest.

"I don't know. Leave me alone," she laughed, nudging me.

"Well, I thought it was cute," I said back to her, sitting up, too. I leaned over to kiss her exposed shoulder, and it made her shrug and giggle.

"Luca," she sighed softly, as I kissed her skin again. At this point I was addicted to the way she breathed my name, and I couldn't help myself.

"I'm sorry, I'm sorry," I said back, kissing her a third time. She giggled again.

"You're not sorry," she said with a smirk on her face, "You do this every morning like we don't have to work." I kissed her lips, climbing on top of her.

"We have time," I said, then paused for a second to look at the time on my phone, "It's 7:15 now, don't have to log in until eight. If you take away the time it'll take you to get dressed and walk down the hall to your apartment, that's like ten minutes, give or take. Which means I have, at least, a good thirty minutes to make sure you start your day off on the right track." She laughed out loud, wrapping her arms around my neck.

"Well, that does sounds nice," she said back, looking up at me with her dreamy eyes. I smiled at her and kissed her again.

"Just tell me where you want me to start," I replied. She giggled again as she pulled the blanket up over our heads, taking me up on my offer.

****

"I meant to ask you this morning why you keep sleeping with this in," Alayah asked me later that day, pointing to my hearing aid, "Isn't that uncomfortable?" I just had logged out of work a few minutes prior, and like clock work, Alayah came back to me.

"Sometimes I just forget to take it out, but I feel like I need it more now," I told her, "I think It's getting worse." Her bottom lip poked out a bit, and her face fell. She walked over to me at my workspace and sat on my knee.

"Don't," I said with a chuckle before she could say anything, "It's okay."

"No, it's not," she said, and squeezed her arms around me so tight I could barely breathe for a second.

"Lay," I laughed, "It has to happen sooner or later. I'm prepared for it." She loosened her hold on me and laid her head on my shoulder.

"Well, I should've became a doctor. Cause then I'd surgically give you my eardrums," she said, and it made me laugh.

"But then *you* wouldn't be able to hear," I reminded her.

"But *you* would," she said back.

"You would do that for me?" I asked, looking at her and she lifted her head again to look at me.

"Of course I would," she replied, "In a heartbeat, if I could."

I could see the sadness in her eyes, even though she tried to smile a little. This was one of the reasons why I loved her from the beginning, she had such a selfless way of thinking, especially when it came to my disorder.

I remembered the hours she spent at my house when we were kids, asking my mom to teach her ASL so she could talk to me no matter what. I remembered the times she came with me to doctors appointments whenever I'd get new aids. If anyone tried to make jokes about it, she was right there with her fists up ready to fight about it, although I never let her. She insisted we go to the same college, "just in case I needed her". I didn't ever need her, but I wanted her, and I was always so glad she was there. I knew it wasn't because she felt sorry for me, but because she cared. She always had. How could I not love her so early in life?

"I wouldn't let you do that," I told her after a while, "You love music too much." Alayah reached up and put her fingers through my hair.

"I would absolutely give up music and dancing and anything else if it meant you could hear it like I do," she said to me. She dropped her forehead on mine, and I held her face in my hand.

"I love you," I told her.

"I love you, too, Luca," she said back. We enjoyed the closeness for a while, but then I broke the silence.

"I wanna do something fun," I said. She smiled a little.

"Like what?" She asked, lifting her head.

"I don't know yet, but I when I figure it out, it'll be fun. I promise," I said, already starting to think of ideas, "Cause technically, I still have to take you on a date."

"Oh my gosh, no," she laughed, standing up from my lap, "We don't have to do that. There's no where to go anyway, all the good places are still closed." I thought for a second, and then an idea crossed my mind.

"Don't worry, I know what we can do."

Chapter 43: Alayah

"I thought I was usually the one who comes up with ridiculous shenanigans," I said to Luca a few days later, as he set up a whole tent in my apartment. He laughed, glancing up at me quickly and then back at his work. We were going camping right in the living room. And thanks to Amazon Prime, we had this giant, forrest green tent in the middle of the floor, along with other unnecessary camping supplies we would probably never use again.

"I guess you've rubbed off on me over the years," he said with another laugh. Then after a few more tugs and pulls and building, the tent was up. Luca stood up and took a deep breath of relief and pride. "Looks great," he said. I laughed at him, sitting cross-legged on the couch that was pushed far back into the kitchen area to make room.

"You're crazy," I teased him.

"Okay," he said, clapping his hands together once, completely ignoring my comment, "S'mores time."

"What?" I laughed out loud, "How!?"

"On the stove, silly goose," he said, walking over to me and messing up my hair like I was a puppy. He continued to the kitchen island, where a Walmart bag sat. He pulled out marshmallows, graham crackers, and Hershey chocolate bars. I got up from the couch and stood next to him.

He turned on the flame on the stove, and put marshmallows on forks, handing me one. I took a fork from him, giggling. We held them over the low flame, the marshmallows browning slowly.

"This is silly," I laughed, rotating the fork over the flame, "Are you gonna tell me a scary story?"

"Do you want me to?" Luca smirked, glancing at me.

"Can't go camping without a scary story," I said back teasingly, a smile curving over my lips. He chuckled a little, and removed the marshmallows from the heat. I watched him in amusement and admiration, as he carefully assembled the s'mores, everything lined up in a perfect order, and he handed me one.

"You'll be too afraid, scaredy-cat," he teased, "Better hope the lights don't go out again." I nudged him, and he laughed at me.

We made a few more s'mores and moved back to the living room. I turned out the lights and the lamps, making it nice and dark. I brought in the blanket from my room and gathered all the pillows I had, and spread them out inside the tent.

Luca had taken my string lights down from the kitchen and hung them on the ceiling in the living room to make them look like stars. With nature sounds faintly playing from his phone, the vibes definitely felt like we were outside. Then, he revealed one more accessory, a lantern light. He was extremely dedicated to this theme, and I thought it was the cutest thing. We both settled into the tent, sitting close, propped up on all the pillows.

"Okay, I doubted you for a second, but this is fun," I said after a while.

"You doubted me? Why?" Luca laughed, "I know it's not much of a first date, but—"

"No, Luca, it's perfect. I love this," I cut him off, reaching over to touch his face. I smiled at him. "You're sweeter than these s'mores," I said to him, and it made him laugh. Then, I kissed him.

"Definitely sweeter," I said again, and he smiled a little.

"That's all you," he said back. I bit my lip trying not to smile as big as I was, but it prompted involuntary giggles instead.

"You're supposed to be telling me a scary story," I said after a moment, and chuckled.

"Okay," he said, turning out the lantern light, making it almost completely dark other than the faint string lights on the ceiling outside of the tent. Then, he turned on the flashlight from his phone, pointing it upwards to cast a shadow over his face. I laughed at the theatrics.

"Once upon a time, there was a guy named Lucas," he started, and I immediately laughed out loud.

"Luca, stop it," I said, nudging him.

"I'm being serious!" He laughed, too, "Do you wanna hear my story or not?"

"Alright, fine," I giggled more, snuggling a pillow under my chin, "Continue."

"So, Lucas had a best friend and her name was Alana," he kept telling me.

"Oh, my gosh," I mumbled, giggling into the pillow to muffle my laughs.

"Please keep all questions and comments until the end, thank you," he said in an announcer voice, and I continued to laugh.

"Alana was the prettiest girl in school, but Lucas was always too scared to tell her how he really felt about her, because he thought she wouldn't be weirded out and wouldn't want to be his friend anymore," he went on.

"I thought this was supposed to be scary," I interrupted again.

"I'm getting there, Alayah!" He shouted back, making me laugh again, "Anyway, in college, Alana started dating this horrid man and it made Lucas sad because he knew he would be better for her than him. He had hope that one day, she would realize that, too, but she didn't. And Lucas was forced to move on with an evil witch, named Riz, who refused to abide by Lucas's basic needs, like learning his preferred language."

"Luca, please," I said, laughing more, amused by this storytelling, "This isn't scary."

"Isn't it?" Luca chuckled a little, "Cause I was terrified living through it." I laughed out loud, tossing a pillow at him. He threw it back, and it turned into a full play fight. Tossing pillows, soft fake punches, tickling and teasing, rolling around and laughing.

"You're gonna knock this tent down that you worked so hard on," I teased, laying under him.

"That's a risk I'll take," he said back with a smirk on his face. Suddenly, the moment turned into something more quiet and intimate as our lips met in a deep kiss.

"Your hands are cold," I giggled, feeling his hand slip under my shirt.

"Sorry," he chuckled a bit, his voice low in my ear. I giggled again as he leaned down to kiss me. The air grew more intense, each touch and each movement fueled by these feelings we had, that were finally out in the open.

Chapter 44: Luca

"Can't believe you lucked out of work," I said to Alayah a few days later, shaking my head as I logged into my computer.

"Thank goodness for system maintenance and towers being down," she smirked, still lying in my bed, "I wish you didn't have to work either. It's a fantastic day to do absolutely nothing."

She kicked the blanket off of her and stood up, my t-shirt on her stopping midway above her knees. She walked over to the window, her bare feet making the hardwood floor creak a little. She opened the curtains, revealing a very cloudy, rainy sky and made a face.

"It's gross outside," she continued. I chuckled a bit, and she walked over to me. I dropped my head back, looking at her standing behind my chair, and she leaned down to kiss me.

"Are you leaving?" I asked her. She shook her head and walked around my chair to stand by the door.

"No, I wanna stay here and bother you all day," she said with a smile, her arms crossing in front of her.

"I was hoping you'd say that," I replied, and her smile got a little bigger.

"Good, because I wasn't leaving regardless," she said, and it made me laugh. Then, she headed through the doorway into the kitchen, "I'm getting cereal, do you want some?"

"Yes, please," I said back to her, turning my attention back to my computer.

And after we ate our quick breakfast, just like she promised, Alayah annoyed me all day long. Of course, I didn't mind. Honestly, I think I was still surprised she loved me back the way I loved her. Her playful and bubbly personality seemed like it had intensified. And experiencing this side of her, this part of her that was soft and endearing, I was just happy I finally had her love. I was enjoying every second of the new attention and love that she showered me with.

When I took my first call, she was quiet, silently poking at me, playing and lightly tugging at my hair, and stealing kisses to purposely rile me up. She thought it was funny, biting her lip as she laughed quietly.

"I'll get you back later," I signed to her, but she just flashed a smirk.

"No, you won't," she signed back, whispering. I raised an eyebrow at her, and she giggled.

When I wasn't on the phone, she'd come sit on my lap and talk to me with her legs and arms wrapped around me. Easily seeing over her head to my screen, I laughed at her antics and her random stories, occasionally stealing back her lips. The rain pelted against the windows, giving a nice background soundtrack to the chill day. By the time my workday was over, it felt like I hadn't worked at all.

"Finally," Alayah sighed exasperatedly just as I turned off my computer. She threw herself backwards on the bed dramatically, "Keeping you entertained all day was exhausting." I laughed at her.

"Keeping me entertained? Is that what you were doing?" I said to her, standing up from my chair, "Or were you entertaining yourself?"

"Both," she replied, giggling. I laid next to her on my back and glanced over at her.

"What do you wanna do now?" I asked her. A smirk curved on her mouth again, and she sat up quickly. Before she could say anything else, I stopped her.

"I'm not ballroom dancing with you again," I said fast, recognizing the mischief in her grin. She immediately burst out laughing.

"I wasn't even gonna say that!" She said back.

"I don't believe you," I teased her, sitting up, too. She laughed more and stood up, her tone shifting a little as she slowly stepped across the room on her toes, exaggeratedly swaying her hips side to side. I chuckled a little bit watching her.

"Take a shower with me," she said softly, stopping in the doorway. I raised my eyebrows and laughed more.

"That's not a good idea," I said to her, looking at the floor and then back at her. If I got in the shower with her, we'd be in there for a long time.

"Why not?" She asked, her voice still the same. She lifted the t-shirt she had on just a little, exposing more of her thighs with this menacing look on her face, "Don't you think it'll be fun?"

"Alayah," I chuckled. She laughed and walked back over, pausing in front of me.

"Am I making you nervous, Luca?" She teased, her hand brushing lightly against my leg. I shook my head, looking up at her laughing. But for some reason, there was a hint of nervousness in there somewhere. There always was. I mean, she was beautiful and her frame was perfect. Didn't really matter how many times I saw her without her clothes, I couldn't help it. And she knew that.

"You're so cute," she giggled, and kissed me. Then, there was a knock on the door. She and I both looked at each other confused. Nobody ever came here.

"Who the heck is that?" Alayah asked and I shrugged.

"I don't know," I said, standing up to go to the door. Alayah followed me over. When I looked through the peephole, I was even more confused than I already was.

"Who is it?" She asked me again. I turned around and sighed.

"Liz."

Chapter 45: Luca

(Continued)

"What are you doing here?" I asked Liz, visibly confused. She stood in front of me with sad eyes, clutching her jacket in her fists.

"I didn't think you'd answer the door," her voice barely squeaked out. Well, I probably shouldn't have. I wasn't going to open the door at all, but Alayah insisted I see what she wanted. She never wanted to come here before, so why was she here now? I stood there, waiting for her to finish talking.

"Luca, I'm sorry," she said, looking at the ground.

"For what?" I asked back.

"Well, I was gonna call first but I didn't expect you to answer that either," she started, looking up again. She paused for a long time, then took a deep breath.

"Luke, I miss you," she finally said, "I want to be with you again. I made a terrible decision and I was wrong. I'm sorry for hurting you."

My eyes squinted and my brows furrowed in disbelief. The entitlement in her voice was almost enraging. Her expression got a little sadder at my reaction, and she looked down again.

"You're not serious. After what you said to me?" I said, but she nodded slightly. I took a deep sigh, "Liz, you can't just show up here and say something like that. You don't have to be sorry, but I don't feel that way at all."

"Luca," she reached for my hand but I moved it, "Can I come in and we can talk about it?"

"Absolutely not," I told her. Even if Alayah hadn't been right behind me, I still wouldn't have let her in.

"Luke, I didn't mean what I said. I was just confused. You're telling me you don't love me anymore at all? Not even a little?" Liz asked, her expression full of hope and desperation at the same time.

"I'm sorry, Liz. I don't," I shook my head. She looked surprised, and her eyes started to water.

"It's only been a couple of months. You moved on already?" She asked me. I nodded.

"What did you expect me to do, Liz?" I questioned, crossing my arms. I felt like my tone was agitated, but I was done trying to be nice to her. I had been done with that a while ago.

"Is she in there now?" She asked me, aggressively wiping a tear from her face. I didn't reply. It wasn't really her business, but I knew that if I told her I was with Alayah that she would automatically assume there had been something going on the whole time.

"Well, sorry I bothered you then," she said, trying to sound upset but she just sounded hurt. Any other time, it would've affected me, but this time I wasn't really fazed. But then she continued, "There's something else I need to tell you, though, before you shut the door in my face."

"Go ahead," I told her, but I wasn't expecting the next thing that came out her mouth. She took a deep breath again.

"I was pregnant, Luke," she said.

I just stared at her, my face going through a range of emotions all at once. It felt like we stood there looking at each other for an eternity as I tried to grasp the full weight of what she just said.

"What do you mean *was*?" I finally managed to ask. I saw guilt wash over her face as more tears fell from her eyes.

"What did you do, Lizzie?" came out of my mouth almost in a whisper, with heavy concern, and I knew it probably wasn't the best thing to ask but I was really struggling to understand.

"Well, I told you a long time ago I didn't want kids. I didn't even know I was until all of this stuff with the virus started," she began rambling quickly, nervously taking her hands through her dark hair, "And I was afraid anyway, because I didn't know what was gonna happen with everybody being sick—"

"Why didn't you tell me?" I asked, my voice raising a little as I stepped further out into the hallway to her.

"Because I knew if I told you, you would've wanted to keep it!" She shouted back at me.

"Lizzie—!" I said, but before I could say anything else, she grabbed my wrist and led me down the hallway to the empty laundry room so we wouldn't keep screaming in the middle of the floor.

"I'm sorry, Luke," she said to me, silent tears still in her pale blue eyes, "I was scared to tell you because I knew you'd be mad at me for what I did. That's why I wouldn't talk to you or call you back. Because, I literally *couldn't* talk to you without thinking about it and feeling guilty about it."

I had no idea what to say. I was lost in a whirlwind of thoughts and emotions. I watched her wipe her tears again and fidget with her jacket again. Any words I might have had completely disappeared.

"You should've told me," was all I could say, "Why wouldn't you tell me, Lizzie?" I walked around the room, trying to unpack everything.

"I did have cold feet a little when you asked me to marry you, because I wasn't sure if I wanted to get married to anyone right now. That wasn't a lie," she said after a while, "But, those other things I said to you weren't true. I only said it because I really didn't know what I was feeling or what I wanted anymore, especially after…that, so I was trying to get you to wanna break up with me. That way it would be easier to do it. But I realized that I'm still in love with you, Luca."

A part of me felt bad because I didn't love her anymore, and the other part of me was angry that she kept something like this from me for so long, and whatever was left over was a jumbled mess of something I couldn't really describe. I wished she would have told me the truth before. But would it have changed anything?

"I'm sorry that I came here without calling first," she continued with a sigh after I still couldn't gather my words, "And whoever you're with now, is really lucky." She started back off down the hallway. For a moment, I just let her go, but then I followed her.

"Lizzie," I called after her, but I still wasn't sure what I was going to say.

"I'm sorry, Luke," she said again, turning around to look at me, her face showed nothing but regret. She turned back around and walked away, giving me one last look before getting on the elevator.

I paced around the hall for a moment before going back into my apartment. Alayah sat on the couch, wearing more of my clothes, sweatpants and a hoodie, with her knees under her chin as she stared at the black screen of the tv. I saw her glance at me, but I didn't want to look back. I knew she heard, at least the important parts. I felt like she was upset. I didn't want to know what she was thinking.

I stopped in the kitchen and leaned over the counter with my head in my hands. I had never felt so many things at once in my whole life, like I got punched in the gut. The silence in the room was heavy for a long time. I still wouldn't look up at Alayah. But then, I felt her gentle touch on me. She wrapped her arms around me from behind and rested her head against my back.

I didn't realize how much I needed the warmth of her hug until then. She didn't say anything, but she didn't have to. I lifted my head and turned around to face her. Her expression matched mine, and she met my eyes hesitantly.

"Are you okay?" She asked me, her hands slowly falling from around me. I nodded slightly, but I don't think she believed me. She hugged me again, a little tighter than before, and we just stood there for a while in the quiet.

237

Chapter 46: Alayah

That night, Luca couldn't sleep. He tossed and turned so much that he eventually just got up and left to sit in the living room. I saw the light from the tv turn on, and heard the muffled sounds from whatever he put on. I didn't know if he knew I was awake, too, or not. I wanted to follow and make sure he was okay, but I figured maybe he just wanted to be alone for a moment. I stared at the ceiling, waiting for him to come back, but he didn't.

By the time I finally decided to check on him, he was asleep on the couch. His phone rested lazily in his hand still, unlocked with a half typed message to Liz still on the screen. I forced myself not to read it. And I didn't really know how to feel. Especially after hearing him call her "Lizzie". He only called her that when he cared, when he loved her.

Over the next few days, he was out of it, despite his best efforts of pretending like he wasn't. There was a distant, contemplative demeanor that was hanging over him. Our normal back-and-forth banter and jokes weren't there. Every conversation we had seemed forced, and it was bothering me.

I tried to shake off my own insecurities, but I couldn't help wondering if he was thinking about Liz and what could've been had she not decided against keeping their baby. The thought of it made my stomach churn with worry and a little bit of envy. I was afraid to talk to him about it, which was silly because I always talked to him about everything and anything. But, this new dynamic between us made something like this so different.

I knew he loved me, but what if this made him miss her? Being in a relationship with someone is one thing, but wanting to marry them is another. And now after this new information? It wouldn't have been far fetched for it to wake up old feelings. And I was terrified. I hated myself for it. I felt like I thinking selfishly, but I couldn't shake it.

"Alayah," he said to me, quietly but with purpose.

"Yeah?" I answered, even quieter. We stood in the kitchen, facing opposite directions as if we were afraid of each other. The rest of his apartment was silent, too, a reflection of the distance between us over the past days.

"What's wrong?" He asked me. I shook my head, even though he couldn't see.

"Nothing, why?" I lied, anxiously tapping my finger tips on the counter.

"Lay, talk to me. What's the matter?" He asked again. I was afraid to bring it up, so I didn't say anything at all.

"Are you mad?" He asked after a moment. I was feeling a lot of things, but anger wasn't one of them. I finally turned around to him.

"Why would I be mad?" I said back. He faced me, too, but didn't look at me.

"The obvious reason," he simply replied.

"I'm not mad, Luca. It's not your fault," I said. He still didn't look up. I sighed and paced around the counter. The heavy tension in the air was a lot.

"This might be a dumb question, but just humor me, okay?" I spoke again after a moment. He shifted his weight from one foot to the other and leaned against the sink.

"Tell me what's on your mind," he prompted.

"Do you still have any feelings for her?" I said through my teeth, still too nervous and afraid to ask in the first place.

"Why would you think that?" He asked, finally looking up at me with concerned eyes.

"The obvious reason," I echoed him, "I don't want you to feel like you chose wrong."

"Alayah, telling you how I feel about you was the best thing I could've ever done. I love you and I love being with you. I just got you, why would I do that to you?" He replied, walking over to me. I just shrugged my shoulders quickly, hoping I didn't sound as ridiculous as I felt.

"I'm just processing," he continued when I didn't say anything, "She should've told me. And honestly, I'm really mad at her for it. I keep feeling like I should reach out to her because I still have a lot of questions, but I know it would be pointless because it doesn't matter now. But I don't want her back."

"I'm sorry that she did this to you," I told him, my voice still quiet.

"*I'm* sorry that I made you feel this way. I didn't mean to," he said back, his expression worried and regretful, and it made me feel horrible about myself.

"No, Luca, you didn't do anything wrong," I told him, reaching up to touch his face, "I'm sorry for being weird and overthinking."

"I hope you know how much I love you," he said to me, pulling me in for a tight hug.

"I love you, Luca," I said back, squeezing him even closer to me.

Chapter 47: Alayah

(Continued)

"You know I don't like doing this with you."

"Shut up. It'll be fun."

"Fun for who? I'm not an artist like you!"

"Just take the knife, Alayah. Actually no, I don't trust you with a knife. Use a spoon."

"How?!"

Luca laughed at me as he cut a hole into the top of the giant orange pumpkin on the kitchen counter. I just stared at my own smaller pumpkin in front of me, waiting for him to share the knife with me. He carefully pulled the stem out and set it beside him. A smile crossed my face.

"Wait, I wanna do it!" I said quickly, and stuck my hands into the pumpkin, pulling out all the slimy insides. I giggled menacingly, twisting and curling my fingers in all the strings and seeds. It was oddly satisfying.

Carving pumpkins was my favorite part of Fall, even though I hated Luca for doing it better than I could. We had been so engrossed in our new relationship that we had completely forgotten about Halloween, and now it was only a week away. So, we ran out to the supermarket and got pumpkins and Halloween themed snacks for a day of fun. We needed it after the unsettling visit Liz pulled last week.

"Ew," Luca said teasingly, watching me. I nudged him, laughing. He walked around me to reach for my pumpkin, and starting cutting into the top of that one, too. We took all the insides out of both, and then Luca handled the knife again.

He meticulously began carving a face into his pumpkin, with triangles for eyes and the nose, and a creepy jagged smile. I admired his skill, knowing mine wouldn't even be close to flawless like his was. When he was done, he stood backwards, looking over his work with a proud smirk.

"Booooo," I joked, "Perfect is boring. Give me that knife. Let the master work." Luca laughed at me again, handing me the kitchen tool. I proceeded to carve my own face, with unpronounced shapes and uneven lines. Luca watched me, doing his very best not to laugh at my off-balanced pumpkin's expression.

"There," I said, dramatically dropping the knife on the counter, "That's a scary face."

"It sure is," Luca chuckled sarcastically. I nudged him again.

I ran over to turn out the lights and placed a small candle into each pumpkin and lit them with a kitchen lighter. The faces flickered with the orange glow, casting shadows on the walls.

"Don't be too afraid, scaredy-cat," Luca teased me, walking towards the living room.

"I'm not a scaredy-cat," I said back, following him to the couch. He chuckled and grabbed the remote, searching for another horror movie to watch. I groaned.

"Do we have to?" I said, laying my head on his lap. He laughed at me again.

"It's not Halloween without horror movies," he said with a smirk.

"It's *not* Halloween yet, actually," I reminded him, "You're five days early." He rested his hand on top of my head, twisting my curls around his fingers as he flipped through movie titles on the tv screen.

"Ooh, Zombies," he said, ignoring me, "Love a good zombie film." I laughed at him.

"You know, as much as you joked about running from zombies before when we talked about the apocalypse, you sure wanna be one so bad," I joked, laughing at him, "The video games, the movies. You'd probably be ecstatic to be turned into one."

"Shut up," he said back, playfully tugging at my hair. I reached up and softly tapped his cheek with my fist. Before another play fight erupted, Luca's phone rang. He took it from his pocket and looked at it. It was his mom.

"Did you tell her yet?" I asked, sitting up straight.

"I did not," he said back, watching it ring.

"That mom instinct is insane," I said, teasing just a little, "Like Spider-Man senses." He did not laugh like I thought he would have.

"I'll be back," he said, standing up from the couch. Then he answered the call finally. He walked into his room and closed the door until it was just barely cracked open. I remained on the couch in the dark, wondering how the conversation was going. I knew his mom would probably feel the same way he did.

The minutes ticked by slowly. I glanced over at the jack-o-lanterns glowing greatly on the kitchen counter, their grinning faces a stark contrast to the tension in the air again. I knew we had talked it out already, but my insecurities still crept back in any time I thought about it. I walked to the kitchen to get a bottle of water to relax my thoughts, turned the lights back on, and then took my seat back on the couch.

Finally, his room door opened again and he came out. I couldn't read his expression. He came over to sit next to me again, and looked over at me.

"Well, that went how it went," he simply said. My face turned into a grimace.

"Yikes, was it that bad?" I asked him.

"Yeah, she's not happy," he said, then chuckled a little, "Just another complaint to add to her list." I thought back to that day when his parents went back and forth bashing Liz, and laughed a bit myself. But then, it faded as I thought about the situation again.

"You're not still mad, are you?" He asked, watching my smile disappear.

"I was never mad at you," I reassured him, fixing my face.

"Are you sure?" He asked again in a singsong tone, leaning a little closer to my face. I giggled a little.

"I'm sure," I told him, taking a sip out of my water bottle, "*She* was the one I was mad at."

"What can I do to make you feel better? You wanna have my kid instead?" He joked. I spit out my water and almost choked from laughter and shock.

"LUCA!" I shouted. He laughed out loud, throwing his head back. "Is it not too early for jokes?" I said to him.

"It's never too early for jokes," he replied matter-of-factly, then continued, "But who said I was joking?" I glanced over at him, trying to hold my giggles in. He looked back at me, raising his eyebrows up and down flirtatiously. I grabbed a pillow from the couch and smacked him lightly with it, right in the face. It sent him into another hysterical laughter.

"Is this a coping mechanism?" I teased him.

"Maybe," he shrugged, laughing, "Maybe not."

"Well, not yet," I said, still teasing, after a while. I watched a smirk curve in the corner of his mouth as a response, and he reached for the remote again.

I glanced at him again while he continued his search for a movie for us to watch. Even though we had just started this relationship, exploring the potential of this new dynamic between us, I thought about it for a second. What if it *was* us instead? If we had a baby, what would they look like? In seconds, I imagined an entire wedding, and kids, and a dog, and a big house with a white picket fence.

I found myself smiling at the possibility of future little me's and little him's running around. Maybe they would have his smile that I loved so much, or his espresso colored eyes. We'd sit around the kitchen table practicing ASL like he and I used to at his house with his mom. Maybe I'd spend the bedtime routine brushing through the curly hair they got from me, or singing songs during bath time because they love music like me. How could Liz not want something like that? I guess, I was glad she didn't.

"What?" Luca asked me, catching me daydreaming.

"Nothing," I said back quickly, but he smiled at me anyway.

"Can I start the movie now?" He asked me, his expression a tad amused at me just staring at him. I nodded and moved closer to him. He smiled, putting an arm around me, pulling me in. I rested my head on him, feeling a strong comfort come over me.

"Come on, scaredy-cat," he said, kissing the top of my head, "I got you." I giggled a little, my body relaxing against his. I looked up at him again, my pupils probably shaped themselves into hearts the way I adored him. He glanced down at me and winked, then looked back at the tv screen.

Chapter 48: Luca

On Halloween, Alayah came out of her room dressed as TinkerBell. The costume fit her well, almost too well and it was exciting me. The short, sleeveless green dress stopped just under her butt and hugged her curves everywhere else. All I could think about was how she looked under it. Her hair had grown a little since she cut it, but she had it pinned up in the character's signature bun perfectly. Small hoop earrings dangled from her ears and a silver necklace lined her neck. I watched her do a little spin with a smile on her face. I was amused by her holiday spirit. She was so happy the pandemic didn't ruin this one for her.

"You know, you could've been an excellent Peter Pan, but you chose to be boring," she said to me while I stood leaning against the couch in my regular clothes. I laughed at that. Despite her begging all week, I refused to dress up with her. I was never into the whole costume thing. Even when we were kids, I didn't dress up then either. Maybe a character graphic t-shirt or crazy hat, but never an actual costume.

"I'm a Lost Boy," I said back to her, folding my arms across my chest.

"And that's exactly what you look like. Lost. Without a costume on Halloween," she replied and it made me laugh out loud again.

"Best I can do is this green t-shirt," I said with a shrug.

"Well, you look sad," she joked, laughing herself.

"You look great, though. Are you sure you don't wanna just stay here?" I suggested, standing up straight. She looked at me, picking up what I was putting down, and smirked.

"Why? You need a little faith, trust, and pixie dust?" She teased, biting her lip, quoting a line from the movie she was dressed as. She walked over to me, batting her eyelashes, and wrapped her arms around my neck. It took a lot of will power for me not to carry her back to her room.

"Okay, relax. Before we really don't go anywhere," I laughed, stepping away from her. She giggled and grabbed her jacket and fairy wings from over by her swivel chair.

"Come on, lover boy," she joked, leading the way out of the door.

We drove to her mom's house in my car. For the last night in October, it wasn't that cold out. It felt like it was almost sixty degrees. Alayah gazed out the window, looking at everyone's Halloween decorations and lights. There were some kids out already, darting across the streets and sidewalks with their getups and jack-o-lantern candy buckets.

Alayah's mom, Stacia, greeted us with a big smile on her face when we got there. Then, she separately greeted me with a hug.

"Wow, I don't get a hug? Cool," Alayah joked, and her mom jokingly pushed her out of the way to hug me again just to spite her. It made me laugh.

"See, this is why I don't come over here," Alayah laughed. She and her mom were just alike when it came to their humor, but that's where the similarities ended.

Other than the big, curly hair Alayah got from her mom, she didn't look anything her. She looked like her dad from what I could remember, but she hated talking about her dad after he left when we were four or five years old. You would've thought she never had one at all the way she pretended he didn't exist. I knew it was just her way of forcing herself to get over it. Her mom used to have to hide old pictures around the house to avoid triggering her. Now, I'm sure she just kept them hidden.

"I see you all the time. I don't see my son-in-law that much," her mom joked back.

"Mother, please," Alayah covered her blushing face.

"I always knew," her mom mumbled with a small smile on her face still, leading the way to the dining room. She pulled out a big round bowl and multiple bags of assorted candy. Alayah helped her open them and fill the bowl up. Then, I followed Alayah back outside where we sat on the porch steps. Kids came and went, happily accepting the treats from her with grins on their faces.

Alayah loved passing out candy. It brought her more joy than actual trick-or-treating did when we were kids, and that was saying something. I remembered every year it was just me and her. Occasionally, we would meet up with her friends, Keaura and Nia, and a couple other classmates we saw around for a while. But we started together and we'd end together, then we would come back here to her mom's living room and watch *Casper The Friendly Ghost* while we sorted through and traded candy.

One year, her ruby red shoe broke—thanks to her cheap Wizard of Oz Dorothy costume—and I carried her on my back for ten blocks all the way back home. I chuckled at the memory.

"What?" Alayah asked.

"Nothing," I shook my head, smiling a little.

"Can you go inside and get another candy bag from my mom? Getting low," she said after a while.

"Yup," I replied, standing up. I headed through the door and back to the dining room where her mom still sat, munching on pieces of candy herself.

"Cleaned out already?" She asked me.

"Yeah, these kids are savages," I joked back. She laughed as she fished out another two bags from a cabinet and handed them to me. I went back outside and dumped all the candy into the almost empty bowl.

"Thank you, baby," she said back, cheesing at me. It caught me off guard a little.

"You're welcome," I laughed at her big smile.

"Can I not call you that?" She asked, a hint of teasing in her voice.

"I didn't say you couldn't," I replied back.

"You're giggling, it made you happy," she teased, poking at my face to make me smile more. I couldn't argue with that.

"Alayah," I laughed, protesting her teasing. She laughed at me and gave me a quick kiss on the cheek.

More kids came up in their route, some assisted by their parents, all excited and in the spirit of the night.

Alayah talked to each one of them individually, smiling and cheerfully commenting to how cute she thought they all looked in their costumes. One little girl skipped up with her mom also dressed as TinkerBell. Alayah jumped up excitedly, showing her they were the same. The little girl got so happy, she hugged Alayah like she knew her and asked her mom to take a picture.

"Do you mind?" The girl's mom asked her.

"Of course not!" Alayah replied happily, and kneeled down to the little girl's height to take multiple pictures per her request.

Such a social butterfly, Alayah was. Always had been. After all the candy was finally gone, she and I returned inside the house. She took her costume wings off and threw on her jacket.

"We should've saved some candy for ourselves," Alayah said, heading towards the dining room. Her mom heard her and smirked as she revealed a hidden stash of more candy.

"I *was* saving it," she smiled proudly.

"Oh, you're the best," Alayah said back, walking over to her.

"You guys can stay for a while if you want. You don't have to rush back home unless you want to," her mom said, handing her a giant candy bag, "I won't bother you. Have a change of scenery for a little." She headed upstairs for the night, and Alayah and I made our way to the living room where there were pumpkin spice scented candles burning on the side tables.

She grabbed the remote, and having the same idea as I did, she rummaged through her mom's old dvds and found one of the movies we used to watch as kids when we were done trick-or-treating. We sat across from each other on the floor and she dumped all the candy out. Mini chocolate bars and gummy bears and rock candy hit the plush carpet. I watched her as she counted out each piece individually so we'd have the same amount.

"Goodnight to all, and to all a good fright," she said right before biting into a Reese's. I laughed at her.

"Still mad you wouldn't be Peter Pan," she said after a second.

"I'm sorry," I chuckled again, "I'll make it up to you on one condition."

"Which is what?" She raised an eyebrow at me.

"Keep that on when we get home," I told her with a smirk. She giggled, covering her face, and she flicked an empty candy wrapper at me.

"Deal."

Chapter 49: Alayah

A few months passed. My twenty-sixth birthday was in November, Luca's in December. All the holidays came and went, and he and I remained in each other's company doing nothing but enjoying the time together. The pandemic was slowly easing, and the world seemed like it was finally opening up once more, especially as the weather warmed up again. There were still plenty of restrictions, but we started venturing out more. We went on actual dates finally, although it made no difference to me. Whether we were still "stuck" inside or being out and about, I was growing to love Luca more and more every day—and I didn't think that was even possible.

We took walks in the park, where the flowers were starting to bloom and the trees were full with new green leaves. I held his hand tight, fingers intertwined, and laughed at him as he pointed out the familiar sights like a National Geographic narrator. His humorous commentary could keep me giggling the whole route around the paths.

"Here we have Alayah out in the wild, in her natural habitat," he joked, forming his hands to hold an invisible camera lens. I laughed out loud, playfully pushing him away from me.

"She's a feisty one, with her lion's mane of curls," he continued, "Be careful not to get too close to this one, folks."

"Hey!" I laughed, nudging him.

And there were endless breakfast, lunch, and dinner dates at our favorite restaurants now that more places were open for indoor seating again. And we shared each other's food and shot jokes across the table and laughed like we were still kids. We went to the movies, and to arcades, and escape rooms, fully taking advantage of the lifted lockdown.

One boring Saturday, we took a trip to a nearby bookstore. There were a few other people there, some sitting at tables silently reading, some checking out books they decided on. The atmosphere was calm and serene, the soft rustling of pages turning and faint scent of paper filled the air. I hadn't been to a bookstore in a long time.

Luca and I lost each other on purpose after a while, indulging in a playful game of pretending to be strangers. I weaved through the aisles, my eyes scanning the spacious room until I saw him. He casually leaned against a wall, a fantasy novel opened in his hand, absorbed in its contents with a concentrated expression on his face. With a shy smile, I walked over to him.

"Excuse me," I said to him, soft but confident, "Hi." He looked up at me, his dark eyes just barely glancing over the rim of his black framed glasses.

"Hi," he said back, trying to suppress a smile.

"What are you reading?" I asked with my arms crossed daintily behind my back, tilting my head slightly as if I was genuinely curious.

"I don't know. The cover caught me so I just flipped to a random page," he replied, still hiding a smirk.

"Well, I didn't mean to bother you. I just think you're really cute, and I wanted to come over and say hi. My name's Alayah," I said, holding up my role. Luca's smile overtook his face as he stood up straight and closed the book.

"Well, I'm glad you did. You're gorgeous," he said back to me, taking my hand in his and kissing it. I giggled uncontrollably.

"Thanks," I replied. We continued back and forth, flirting and laughing quietly, creating our own little world amidst the chill atmosphere of the store.

After a while, it was his turn to find me. I casually browsed through the books on the shelves, a few of them interesting me for real. I spotted a black-covered book with shiny purple writing on the spine. I reached up on my toes to the top shelf to grab it, my fingers just inches away. Then, Luca stepped in, reaching up effortlessly, and grabbed the book for me.

"Thank you. I was struggling," I said, smiling up at him.

"You're welcome," he replied, handing me the book. With a charming smirk and a slightly mischievous glint in his eyes, he added, "I've never seen you here before. Do you come here often?"

"Sometimes," I tried not to giggle as I fidgeted with the book in my hands, "It's been a while." I shifted, my back against the shelves.

He nonchalantly leaned forward, his arm propped on the shelves behind me. I looked up at him, and his eyes glanced over me slowly, playing this role a little too well or forgetting it completely.

"Can I help you with something?" I asked him, shyly.

"Sorry," he chuckled a little, "I got distracted by your dreamy eyes." The giggles escaped my mouth anyway, and my cheeks got hot.

"You think my eyes are dreamy?" I asked him. He nodded like I should've already known.

"I could look into them all day," he said. He leaned closer, and this silly little game was forgotten for a moment as he gently grabbed my face and kissed me.

"You can't just walk up to strangers and kiss them," I teased, my voice soft and quiet as our faces lingered close.

"Sorry, I couldn't help myself," he replied, then kissed me again. I doubt the other people in the store even noticed us in this interaction, too engrossed in their own reading, but the moment felt like it lasted forever. And I still didn't want it to end.

"Can we go home?" I asked him after we finally parted lips. He smiled a little and laughed low in my ear before kissing me again.

"Come on," he said finally. I giggled some more as he grabbed my hand and lead us through the bookstore. We ran back to his car and drove back to our apartment building, way too excited to get home and be alone again.

Chapter 50: Luca

By the time it was May again, Alayah and I finally decided to cut out the walking back and forth down the hall to each other's apartment, and just live together. I mean, it just made sense anyway. We never slept alone anymore, and we could only be in one place at a time, so it was an easy decision. We moved from the third floor to the second into a slightly bigger apartment that fit everything comfortably.

The process of merging our lives into one space was exciting, although it wasn't hard. Over the last months, we slowly and absently moved things into each other's apartments anyway. We kept some things and got rid of others, making it a nice blend of both of our stuff.

The living room was Alayah's favorite part. It was spacious enough for her to dance her little heart out whenever she wanted, the hardwood floor were perfect for her to move freely, and the big windows let in plenty of natural light. We kept her couch and swivel chair, they were better than my old futon anyway.

The kitchen was a noticeable improvement from our previous ones. It was also a bit bigger with more counter space and newer appliances, although Alayah constantly voiced how she missed the center island, where she always practiced her "bartending" skills.

Alayah made sure our shared bedroom was cozy with her many blankets and throws and pillows. The second bedroom we transformed into a dual workspace for our work-from-home jobs. Her desk was closest to the window, decorated with colorful stickers and magnets, multicolored sticky notes plastered all over her computer, and rainbow pens lined up at the keyboard. Mine was its usual minimalist setup, just a few essential gadgets and writing tools.

Everything had its place and I loved every second of officially living together. But there was one morning that left things a little shy of perfect. I woke up to Alayah gently shaking me. As my eyes opened, I saw her face filled with concern and confusion.

"Hey. Luca? Can you hear me?" I watched her mouth form the words but all I heard was silence. She spoke more, but I heard nothing. I tried not to panic as I stood up quickly, pulling and scratching and rubbing at my ears like I was trying to make them work. I had never felt this type of silence before. It was heavy, almost tangible, almost as if it had its own sound—an extremely overwhelming absence of noise that was mocking.

I mean, of course I knew this day was on its way, especially as it seemed my broken ears were getting worse over the last several months, but it was still a bit of a shock. I thought I would've had a *little* more time before my hearing disappeared for good. Actually, I think deep down I believed it would have never happened to begin with, but I guess not.

Alayah watched me pace around as if she didn't know what to do. I mean, what could she do? There was nothing to do. Finally, she got up and walked over to me, realizing I was struggling. The worry disappeared from her face, and she just wrapped her arms around me and stayed there for a long time. Then, she looked up at me.

"It's okay. I'm here," she signed, but somehow it didn't make me feel better.

Chapter 51: Alayah

I don't think I had ever seen Luca cry in my entire life before that moment. I was not fond of it either. I don't know what I thought his reaction might have been when this day came, but he was taking it hard. It was also the first time in years that I saw him use both hearing aids at the same time. Even with them in, he wouldn't say anything. He didn't want to talk or do anything. Any time I tried to get close enough to offer some type of comfort, he moved away from me. I felt helpless.

I knew he didn't mean to be distant, but it broke my heart watching him go through this, feeling like I couldn't do anything. He grasped at anything for noise, turning both tvs on in the living room and our bedroom at max volume, playing music from his phone, over exaggerating any type of footstep or movement, rustling through the silverware and dishes. It was a little overstimulating for me, and strange behavior for him, but I knew he needed it so I didn't say anything. I sat in our room for most of the day, giving him whatever space he wanted.

That night, I noticed him attempting to sleep with both aids in. He was uncomfortable and I could tell. He hadn't spoke a word to me all day, but I placed a gentle hand on his shoulder.

"Hey, you can take those out," I said to him, hesitantly, "I'll wake you up when you want me to."

"No, I wanna keep them in," he said back dryly, not looking at me. I sat up and faced him.

"Luca, I don't want you to be restless all night. Give yourself a break from these—"

"Can you stop?" He snapped at me, his voice raised, "I said I wanna keep them in."

"I'm just trying to help. I'm not trying to make you mad," my voice way quieter than before, a little shocked and hurt that he would yell at me.

"Then, stop," he shot back, "I said I got it. I don't need your help right now." He turned away from me and it was quiet. I sunk back under the blanket and faced away from him, too. With silent tears in my eyes, I did my best to fall asleep. Upsetting him was not my goal and I was sorry that I had. I was sad for him and this struggle he was in.

****

In the morning , he didn't say two words to me, and I didn't want to say anything either. I was too afraid he was still mad from last night. But after a while, he grabbed his car keys from the kitchen counter and headed for the door. I followed him.

"Hey," I said, catching him by his arm, then spoke and signed at the same time, "Where are you going?"

263

"To my parents's house," he replied, not signing at all.

"I'll go with you," I said.

"No," he said back quickly, "I'm fine." He turned back towards the door, but I stopped him again.

"Luca."

"I don't need you to come with me. I got it," he said harshly, same tone as last night. I tried not to let it hurt my feelings again, but he sighed seeing the expression on my face.

"I'll be back later," he said in a more relaxed tone.

"When is later?" I asked, concerned. I didn't want to be naggy or pushy, but I was worried about him. Just because we were together now, it didn't stop him from being my best friend. He dropped his head back and sharply exhaled.

"Alayah, please," he stressed.

"Just let me come with you or I'll worry about you the whole time you're gone," I told him, stepping closer to him. The last thing I wanted was to stress him out more, I wasn't trying to. I just hated seeing him so upset.

"I don't want need you to worry about me, Lay. I can function without you," he shot back. My eyebrows furrowed.

"I have never treated you like you couldn't function without me. Why would you say that?" I replied, my voice cracked into a lower tone.

"You always have," he said accusingly, "Just because my ears are broken doesn't mean I can't do things by myself."

My expression was probably a mix of confusion and shock and a little bit of anger. He had never said anything like that before. He couldn't have meant it. At least, I hope he hadn't. And I *hated* when he referred to his ears as "broken". It made me sad. I didn't even know what to say back.

"Listen, Alayah. I don't wanna fight with you right now," he said quietly, stressfully running his fingers through his hair, "I love you, I do, but you gotta give me a second, okay? Just give me a couple hours." I just nodded. We left it at that and he went out the door. And once again, I felt helpless.

Chapter 52: Luca

As much as I knew Alayah just wanted to help, there was no way she possibly could. She didn't understand, and she would never understand. Not fully. So, I went to the only person I knew that could, which was my mom of course. I told her I was coming, so the front door was already unlocked when I got there. I just about burst through the door, my steps heavy and hurried. Although, I wasn't sure what my rush was.

My mom sat in the living room, watching some old drama, but she turned around to me when she heard me coming. She immediately noticed the distraught expression on my face.

"Luca, what's wrong?" She asked, signing at the same time with instant concern in her voice. I opened my mouth to speak, but my eyes burned with tears I didn't really want to let out. A storm of emotions swirled around in my head. I sat next to her on the couch.

"It's gone," I managed to get out, trying to steady my voice, "I can't hear anything on my own at all. It's gone."

"Oh, Luca," she sighed, her face collapsing with empathy, "Come here." She pulled me into a warm, comforting embrace. Any other time, I would've argued that I was too old for a hug like this from my mom, but at that moment, it was exactly what I needed.

After a while, she let me go and looked at me with understanding. She took a deep breath, her hands moving as she signed while she spoke.

"I was your age, too, when my hearing went away completely, maybe a couple years older," she said, "I know exactly how you feel right now. It does get easier to get used to, especially when you have people around you who understand and care and love you."

My mind drifted to Alayah, and I felt a little guilty for snapping at her before I left. I didn't mean any of it. I felt horrible for taking my frustration out on her. I exhaled heavily, feeling the weight of her sad face just as I shut the door. I wasn't planning on being so upset, but this one time I just needed some space.

"You're not alone, Luke, but I know you know that already," my mom's soft-spoken voice broke the silence again, "And it's okay to give yourself time, too. But whatever you need, your dad and I are always here." I nodded, some of my emotions easing just a bit.

"Can I stay here?" I asked her after a while.

"Of course, you can. You don't have to ask," she replied with a small, comforting smile. She stared at me for a moment, and tilted her head in curiosity.

"Are you and Alayah okay?" She asked, reading my face too perfectly. I glanced at her quickly, then down at the floor.

"Probably not," I answered honestly with a shrug, thinking back to earlier again. My mom poked her lip out a little.

"She loves you so much, Luke," she said to me, placing a hand on my shoulder.

"I know," I said with a sigh, some frustration coming back, "I just hate when it feels like she feels sorry for me or something. I don't like that." A wave of perplexity came over my mom's face, and she turned to face me more.

"When has she ever made you feel that way?" She asked me, almost like she didn't believe it. I really didn't have an answer for her question. Her expression changed again, curiosity and knowingness both at the same time.

"Are you sure that's the issue?" She asked me. I hated that she saw through me.

For some reason, in my tornado of emotions, there was a small fear that Alayah would decide she didn't want to be with me anymore because of this. I guess it had always been in the back of my mind that she couldn't possibly want to be with someone who's ears didn't work, no matter how long we had been friends. And now that my eardrums were double dead, that concern came back full force. It wasn't that I thought she felt sorry for me. *I* felt sorry for *her*, for having to deal with me and my disability.

Of course, I never told her that. I knew what she would say, and I knew it wouldn't have changed the way I felt. It was the reason I had avoided her all day, and the reason I didn't want her to come with me. I didn't want her to feel like she had to because I needed her help now. After voicing all of that to my mom, she poked her lip out again.

"That breaks my heart that you feel that way, Luke," she said, "but do you really think she feels that way?" I didn't answer her again, so she kept going, "You have never been dependent on anyone your entire life. I think you've handled it way better than I did. I know those kids in school made it hard sometimes, the way they would tease you. But you never let it get to you, and you always seemed happy because you had such a good friend by your side. Alayah would never think that way." I knew she was right, but I still couldn't help feeling the way that I was.

The rest of the day passed slowly at my parents's house. I hadn't realized how much time dragged without Alayah next to me, but I didn't want to go home just yet. I still needed some time to process everything.

As the night came, the house grew quieter. My mom and dad were in the living room, eating dinner together. I wasn't hungry, even though I hadn't eaten anything all day. I settled in my old room, which was now just a plainly decorated guest room, and just stared at the ceiling as I laid down. I took both my hearing aids out, trying to let myself get used to the complete silence. But the quiet mixed with the darkness of the night was oppressive and overwhelming, and I realized how much I missed Alayah.

Chapter 53: Alayah

Luca walked through the door the next morning at nine. The worry that quite literally kept me up all night bubbled into frustration. I didn't want to be *that* person, but after dealing with my ex, Cameron, for so long, I was an over-thinker. And I wasn't fond of the scenarios my brain had come up with all throughout the night.

The morning light streamed through the living room windows, casting a yellow glow on the furniture. I stood in the kitchen, my nails gripping the edge of the counter as I tried to ignore the many emotions I felt. The coffee machine brewed next to me. I barely liked coffee but after not sleeping, I needed it.

Luca stepped in, looking exhausted and remorseful. Our eyes met briefly before I looked away. I turned to grab a mug from the cabinet, and poured the coffee in with deliberate slowness. I couldn't tell if he was walking to me or past me, but I did him a favor and headed into our room before I could find out. But before I got in, he gently caught my arm and I stopped in my tracks. I paused and took a deep breath, placing my mug down on the counter again. I finally looked up at him.

"I'm sorry," he said. I could see the weariness in his eyes, the guilt etched on his face. My anger disappeared just a little.

"Why didn't you tell me you weren't coming home?" I asked. I wanted to sound firm, mean even, but I looking at his face, I just couldn't. My voice came out like a mouse. He took a long time to answer, and I didn't like that. But I tried to remember that this was Luca in front of me, not Cameron.

"The longer I stayed at my parents's house, I just didn't wanna leave. I talked to my mom all day. I needed somebody who knew how I was feeling," he explained, his tone timid and soft.

"Okay, I understand that," I said, calmly, "but why didn't you call me? Or just text me if you didn't wanna talk?"

"I don't know," he sighed heavily, then said again, "I'm sorry, Alayah." It was quiet for a while as we stood there.

"Are you mad at me?" He asked after the long pause. I took a deep breath.

"No," I replied.

And I wasn't really mad. I was sad he was shutting me out. He had never done that to me before. He stared at me for a moment, searching my eyes to see if I was lying or not. He let out a sharp exhale and stepped backwards a little.

"This is harder than I thought it would be," he said, his jaw clenched slightly, "I didn't think I would feel this way." Every emotion I felt prior to that disappeared, and more sadness took over.

"You have every right to feel how you do. I'm sorry for pushing, it's just...you know how I am. I worry about you because I love you, ever since we were little," I didn't realize I was crying until he wiped a few tears away from my cheek, "I just wish it were me instead of you."

"You don't mean that," he said to me, but I nodded quickly.

"Yeah I do. I told you before. If I could switch places with you right now, I would," I told him, more tears falling and my nose sniffling, "I'd do anything for you, Luca."

"I'd do anything for you, too. Except let you do that," he said with a little smile, but it only made more tears come. I hugged him so tight, we both almost lost our balance. He wrapped his arms around my shoulders protectively, holding my head close to his chest. My tears dried up, being in his embrace.

"I'm sorry I didn't call. I'm sorry for being mean and yelling at you. I don't wanna be mean to you. I love you so much," he said to me, "I guess I'm just a little afraid."

"Afraid of what?" I asked him, popping my head up to look at him.

"I don't wanna lose you, Lay," he said as if my sadness passed over to him.

"Why would that happen?" I asked, confused. His arms dropped from around me and took big a breath.

"I don't want you to get tired of this, or realize that it's not what you want," he started, pacing around the room, "When things go back to normal all the way with this pandemic, I don't want you to change your mind about me.

Maybe you only have feelings for me because you had to, because we were stuck together. And when you start being with your friends more and going out again, you might realize you don't want me or my broken ears anymore. Especially now."

I processed his words, completely unbelieving that he would ever think such a thing. As if I wasn't sad enough already in that moment. I watched his face turn so heavily melancholy at the thought of his own words, and I just threw my arms around him again.

"Luca, I love you," I said, looking at him and holding his face in my hands, "Being your friend was amazing enough, but being with you is a thousand times better. I could never change my mind about you, babe. I am so sorry that you felt that way but it is not true. Not even a little bit." His mouth curved into a small smile, and he looked back at me with so much love in his eyes that I could feel it.

"And stop calling your ears broken. I hate that," I added, "They're not broken. They're cute. Now, stop it." He laughed genuinely. I wasn't trying to be funny, but I was glad it made him feel better.

"I love you, Lay," he said after a moment.

"You better, after I was up all night," I said back, playfully punching his arm. He laughed again and pulled me close to him by my waist and kissed my lips.

"I'm sorry," he said again, "If it makes you feel any better, I didn't sleep either."

"Sounds like a nap is in order," I responded, raising my eyebrows in suggestion.

"I could go for a nap," he nodded in agreement, smiling a little.

"Same, let's go," I said, and he laughed. I grabbed his hand and led the way into our room. We laid close to each other, cozy under the blankets, and soon drifted off into a well needed sleep.

Chapter 54: Luca

A few days later, I went to my audiologist doctor for upgraded, more effective hearing aids. I hadn't been there in a while, because of the pandemic of course, but lucky me it wasn't hard to get a quick appointment. I had the same audiologist since I was a kid, so this visit was already something we knew was coming and had planned for. Alayah went with me, she always did whenever she could. She used to tag along with my parents when we were little when they would take me. Having that support from her still made me feel a bit better.

I sat in the waiting room of the doctors office, my hands fidgeting with slight nervousness. Alayah sat beside me, tapping her foot to the faint music playing overhead. She noticed my uneasy hands and placed her hand on top of mine, without even looking over. The gesture calmed me only for a moment.

When I got called back, I took a deep breath and stood up. Alayah followed close behind me. The audiologist, Dr. Martinez, greeted us both with a smile. It had been a couple years since I had been here, but she still remembered me and Alayah both.

"How are you?" She asked me, signing in ASL too, as she led us into a room, where familiar equipment and charts lined the walls. I didn't really have an answer, so she rephrased her question.

"How have you been coping? I guess is what I should say," she said.

"It's been…interesting," I finally replied. She gave me an understanding glance.

Dr. Martinez also had a genetic hearing disorder, slightly different than mine, but for the most part, she knew how I felt, too. Her custom aids sparkled with purple glitter in her ears every time she turned her head.

"Yeah, that's normal," she said, her tone compassionate, "When I lost my hearing, I was thirteen. My parents had to carry me into my doctor's office. Dramatic little me couldn't even walk in the building." She laughed a little and Alayah did, too.

"Alright, let's see," she said, grabbing her tools. As the doctor started all the necessary examinations, Alayah stayed close to me, paying attention to every little thing Dr. Martinez did and occasionally asking questions.

Afterwards, the doctor officially confirmed what I already knew and discussed next steps. There was talk of cochlear implants, which is what my mom had, but I wasn't sure I wanted to go through a whole surgery. At least, not now. My mind just wandered, processing the finality of my condition.

As Alayah and I left the office, I felt a small sense of relief having newer, more effective aids on the way. And with Alayah with me, it was kind of hard to stay down for long. She held my hand tightly as we walked through the parking lot to her car. She got into the driver's seat and looked over at me.

"Are you okay?" She asked me. I nodded and took a breath.

"Yeah, I'm fine," I told her and this time I meant it, "Thanks for coming with me." She smiled and reached over, gently scratching through the stubble on my face.

"I love you," she said to me, her voice soft.

"I love you, too," I said back. She dropped her hand and started the car.

"Wanna go eat?" She suggested, a hopeful smile crossing her face.

"Of course, I wanna go eat," I told her, and she laughed. She pulled out of the parking and started down the road.

****

"Hey," I said to Alayah a week later, walking over to her in the living room, "Get dressed." She had been sitting on the couch, cross-legged, with a book in her hands while I finished up work. She looked up at me and pushed her glasses up her nose.

"Get dressed for what?" She asked and signed simultaneously.

"I'm taking you somewhere," I told her, leaning on the couch to look over her shoulder to see what she was reading.

"Where?" She asked, her eyes lighting up with curiosity.

"Do you always have to ask so many questions?" I laughed a little. She closed her book and turned her body to face me.

"Well, yeah," she laughed, too, "I have to know what I'm dressing for."

"Just wear something nice," I told her. She looked at me like she was wondering what I was up to, but I wanted it to be a surprise. I still felt bad for being harsh with her the other day, so I wanted to do something for her. One of the theaters in the city was putting on a live show of one of her favorite musicals, and I couldn't wait to see her face when I took her there.

"Okay," she finally agreed, "What time are we leaving?" I thought for a second, then glanced at my phone for the time.

"In a hour and a half?" I said.

"I can do that," she smiled. She stood up and walked around the couch to me, quickly giving me a kiss on the cheek before ducking into the bathroom for a shower.

As we both got ready for the night, we passed each other back and forth through the apartment, still talking as we zipped around each other. Alayah, of course, played music from the tv as she got dressed, singing quietly in between conversations with me.

"Lay," I called for her, as I waited for her in the living room after I was done.

"I'm coming!" She laughed from the bathroom, already knowing what I going to say. I chuckled at her and shook my head, pacing around the room as if it would make the time go faster.

"How do I look?" She asked me, finally emerging. I glanced up at her and was stuck for a moment, looking at how beautiful she was.

She wore all black, a short flaring skirt and a thin cropped matching sweater that accentuated her figure. I hadn't seen her wear heels in a long time, but they made her legs look even more elegant and graceful than she already was. Her hair, that had returned to its long length by then, was pulled back from her pretty face, the distinct curls flowing down her back. She fumbled with the necklace around her neck, waiting for my answer. But "wow" was all I could say. She giggled a little.

"Is that it?" She asked walking over to me, trying to hide a smile, "I'm not overdressed, am I?"

"No, not all," I told her, still in awe of her beauty, "I don't think there's a word invented for how gorgeous you are." A bigger smile took over her face and she looked down at her feet.

"Luca's poetic now," she teased, looking back up at me. I laughed a little. "You look handsome," she added, grazing the collar of my shirt with her fingertips.

"Thank you, love," I responded, and she giggled again, "Are you ready?"

"Are you gonna tell me where we're going?" She asked back as I grabbed my car keys.

"Nope," I replied with a smile. I reached my hand out for her and she took it, looking at me with mock irritation for not telling her the surprise just yet. We headed out the door and down the hall. She held my hand as we rode the elevator down to the main floor.

The sun was going down, but it was still warm out. I opened the car door for her, and she smiled at the gesture as she graciously slid into the passenger seat. As we drove, I stole glances at her and she stole them right back.

"Where are we going?" She asked me again as we drove further away from town. A smirk crossed my face and I shook my head.

"I'm not telling you," I said back.

"Ugh, Luca," she laughed. I placed a hand on her thigh.

"Don't worry your pretty little head about it," I said jokingly, "We'll be there soon."

Finally, we pulled up to the Grand Theater in the city. I found a decent spot to park in, and we got out. Alayah held onto my arm as we walked through the large parking lot, still blissfully unaware of what we were doing. As we approached the entrance, she caught sight of the glowing marquee displaying the name of her favorite musical. She gasped and turned to me in disbelief.

"Shut up!" She exclaimed, excitedly slapping at my arm, "No way!" I laughed at her, amused and happy at her reaction. I felt a sense of accomplishment, showing her the tickets I pulled from my pocket. The glow from the theater lights reflected in her eyes as her grin grew.

"Why are you like this? Why are you so cute?" She said to me, looking up at me with love in her eyes. I chuckled again, leading her into the building.

"Cause I love you," I told her, squeezing her hand. She smiled at me, and stopped our stride to hug me.

We settled in our balcony seats, Alayah still cheesing ear to ear being so high up where she could see the whole theater. She marveled at the ornate decorations and the shining glass chandelier hanging from the ceiling. Murmurs of the audience added a buzz of anticipation that matched her excitement. Soon, the lights dimmed and the show began. The orchestra started to play music loud enough to vibrate through the room. The curtain rose, and so did Alayah's eyebrows as her face lit up.

As the production went on, I watched her instead. She knew every word of dialogue by heart, and her real singing voice rang through as she sang along to all the songs. The joy on her face was unmatched, and I was happy seeing her happy. When it was over and the curtains closed again, she cheered the loudest, clapping and smiling so big, I thought she was going to burst. And I still just watched her, admiring her in her happiness.

Chapter 55: Alayah

"That was the best experience I've ever lived through," I said to Luca as he carried me on his back down the hall to our apartment, my heels dangling from my right hand, and my left arm around his neck.

"Oh, really?" Luca asked back with a laugh, a hint of mock offense in his voice.

"Okay, well, you know what I mean!" I laughed. "The best experience I've ever lived through besides being with you," I added, then kissed his cheek. He put me down when we got to the door, and took his key out to unlock it.

I followed him in, then grabbed his hand. I turned in circles, singing lines from the show. Luca rolled his eyes and laughed at me, but he didn't protest like usual. He pulled me into him, automatically assuming dance position: hand on my waist and the other holding my hand close to him.

"Ooh, smooth," I said to him, impressed, "I'm rubbing off on you finally after all these years?" He chuckled again and kissed my nose, which made me giggle.

"Maybe," he said back.

I smiled at him and put my arms around his neck. He picked me up again so that I was facing him this time. He kissed my lips just before setting me down on the kitchen counter. I stared at him for a moment, admiring his handsome face and thinking about how much I had grown to love him in the past several months.

"Luca?" I said after a second, my hands still resting on his shoulders.

"Hmm?" He met my eyes.

"When did you know that you were in love with me?" I asked him.

"I thought we talked about this before?" He said, a little surprised by my question. I shook my head slightly.

"No, you just said a long time. You didn't say when it started," I told him. He laughed a little and thought for a second.

"I've always loved you, Alayah," he said finally, making perfect eye contact, "I don't think I can pinpoint a specific day. You've always been selfless, and funny, way more out going than me." I laughed at that a little.

"You're beautiful," he continued, his voice soft and sweet, "Vibrant. You've always been here for me when I needed you, even when I thought I didn't need you. You're my best friend, Lay. How could I not love you?"

"You're so sweet," I said back, holding his face in my hands for a second, "I just wish you would've told me sooner." He nodded.

"Yeah, me too," he said with a short laugh, "I could've saved us both from a lot of heartbreak."

"Ugh, I wish you would have!" I laughed, thinking about all the relationships and breakups that we had been through with other people throughout the years. I thought about all the heartbreaks and tears and venting and ranting to each other, and wondered if everything would have been so much easier if we had just been with each other from the start.

"It's like, I missed you or something," I added, "I don't know how to explain it, but it's so easy to love you." He smiled, then he met my eyes again.

"Being loved by you is an amazing feeling," he said, leaning closer to me. Our lips met, short and sweet, but still warm and soft.

"I want a better kiss than that," I said, teasingly. He laughed.

"Are you done talking?" He asked me, "Cause if you're not, then I have to wait. If I kiss you again, I won't stop unless you tell me to."

"Well then, in that case," I giggled, pulling him close again, "I'm done talking."

Chapter 56: Luca

Alayah and I sat out in the common area, enjoying a nice day. The warm sun and blue sky, a few wispy clouds drifting by. She laid on her back in the grass on her favorite throw blanket, her curls spiraled out around her. I was next to her, my eyes fixated on her face as she closed her eyes and smiled a little. I thought about the past year and all the chaos that had taken place.

"What's on your mind?" She said to me while signing. Her skin shimmered in the sun's rays, her dreamy brown eyes squinting at the bright light of the day as she looked up at me.

"You," I told her, and she laughed a little.

"How can you think about me and I'm right here?" She asked amused.

"You're always on my mind, Lay. I told you that before," I said back. She smiled, and pulled me down to the ground with her with a playful roughness.

"You're so cute," she said to me, then started kissing me all over my face, her soft lips brushing against my cheeks, forehead, and nose. I laughed at her sudden wave of affection. She rested her head on my shoulder, using my arm as a pillow.

"Hey, do you remember when we first moved into these apartments?" She asked me after a while.

"You'll never let me forget," I replied, shaking my head.

"When we got stuck elevator?" She said, a burst of laughter sounding from her.

"That was not fun," I told her, laughing, too as the memory came back to me.

"Oh, shoot! I broke it," Alayah hysterically laughed at herself as the elevator shook and stopped completely.

"Why would you press all the buttons at one time? You goof," I said back to her, placing the boxes I had in my hands down on the floor.

"I've done it before. This never happened!" She laughed more.

"Yeah, in like a hospital or hotel or somewhere with updated equipment. Not in this old apartment building," I said back. I sighed, putting my face in my hand. "We should've taken the stairs again," I added.

"Okay, relax," she said back, with an assuring hand in my shoulder, "I'll text my mom and tell her to call the landlord." She pulled out her phone, and her positive expression shifted.

"Ooh," she said with a grimace, "No service."

"I could've told you that," I glanced at her, slightly irritated. We had been up and down the stairs for hours, with the help of my parents and her mom. We only had a

few more little things to carry in, so we took the elevator to
be quick. But here we were.

"Okay, emergency button. Do us some good," she
said to herself as she tapped the bright red button on the
wall. But nothing happened.

"I'm gonna kick your butt, Lay," I joked, "When we
get out of here, I'm beating you up."

"I'm sorry!" She howled in laughter again.

For hours, we paced around the small, square
small, sending text messages that never seemed to go
through. We sat, occasionally pushing the emergency
button again just in case. Alayah attempted a game of I-
Spy, which didn't last long at all.

"Okay, I give you permission to beat me up," she
said, laying her head on my shoulder. I shook my head at
her, and chuckled a little. Finally, the elevator whirred up
again, shook a little, and then started to move.

"Thank God," I mumbled, standing up. The
elevator doors opened up, and Alayah and I quickly
gathered the boxes and headed down the hall. Our parents
were waiting for us in front of our old apartments.

"Can't wait to keep annoying you," Alayah said,
nudging me, "And now I'll only be a few steps away to do
it." I glanced over, her facing curving into a big grin, and
laughed at her again.

"I meant that, you know," Alayah said to me, "I like
annoying you."

"You love annoying me almost as much as you love
loving me," I said teasingly. She laughed, sitting up.

"Is it that obvious?" She teased back, in a semi
sarcastic tone. I laughed and sat up to look at her face.

"Jokes on you because you could never annoy me," I said back to her just like I had at the beginning of all this, "But I want you to keep trying for as long as you can." She met my eyes and smiled softly.

"I love you, Luca," she said, holding my face in her hand. Her smile grew a little bigger, a little more menacing, and added, "You and your cute broken ears." I laughed out loud, falling backwards again.

"You said you hated when I said that!" I laughed.

"It's different when I do it," she teased, laying her head back on me. We stayed outside for a while, still laughing and talking. I thought about everything again.

The pandemic was far from over, even though things were slowly becoming more normal again, but it had definitely turned everything upside down. The isolation, Alayah's messy breakup, whatever that was that Liz pulled, and the inevitable stage of my hearing loss. As crazy as it was, it all led right back to Alayah and the feelings I had for her from the very beginning. If someone had told me beforehand I'd finally have her, I probably wouldn't have believed it, but I was so happy that it was real.

The End

CHECK OUT MY OTHER NOVELS
"If I Can Find You"
"If I Can Keep You" -A Sequel to the above
"Sent For Me"
"Eye for an Eye"
and "My Brother's Best Friend"

And please follow & like my Facebook page: Dashia Renee
Williams' Books
Thank you for reading!